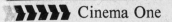

5 Westerns

Illinois Central College
Learning Resources Center

Westerns
spects of a Movie Genre

ilip French

he Viking Press
ew York

PN
1995
.9
.W4
F7
1974

The Cinema One series is published by
The Viking Press, Inc., in association with
Sight and Sound and the Education
Department of the British Film Institute.

Copyright © 1973 by Philip French

Published in 1974 in a hardbound and paperbound
edition by
The Viking Press, Inc.,
625 Madison Avenue, New York, N.Y. 10022

SBN 670-75727-6 (hardbound)
        670-01972-0 (paperbound)

Library of Congress catalog card number: 73-8480

Printed and bound in Great Britain

Contents

Cover: *The Culpepper Cattle Company*

John Ford's *The Searchers*

I think nowadays, while literary men seem to have neglected
their epic duties, the epic has been saved for us, strangely
enough, by the Westerns . . . has been saved for the world by of
all places, Hollywood.

> Jorge Luis Borges
> *The Paris Review*, 1967

One of the most vapid and infantile forms of art ever conceived
by the brain of a Hollywood movie producer.

> Dwight Macdonald
> *The Miscellany*, 1929

The XXth Congress had taken place, but there wasn't a line
about the speech. It wasn't in any of the later papers either, and
by and by I realised that it had not been meant for us. Well
there were newspapers on sale two hundred yards beyond the

order, next to wooden booths with all the rubber bands in the world, and tomatoes, and Hollywood westerns that don't exist on our side either; the text of the speech was still around.

Uwe Johnson
Speculations About Jakob, 1959

The Western remains, I suppose, America's distinctive contribution to the film.

Arthur Schlesinger
Show, April 1963

What recent films have you found particularly stimulating?

The Searchers, *Moby Dick*, *The Red Balloon* – and almost every film in which the heroes are white, the villains red and the United States cavalry gets there in time.'

The Rt. Hon. Peter Rawlinson, MP,
replying to a questionnaire on
the cinema in *Sight and Sound*, 1957

Other people, so I have read, treasure memorable moments in their lives: the time one climbed the Parthenon at sunrise, the summer night one met a lonely girl in Central Park and achieved with her a sweet and natural relationship, as they say in books. I too once met a girl in Central Park, but it is not much to remember. What I remember is the time John Wayne killed three men with a carbine as he was falling to the dusty street in *Stagecoach*, and the time the kitten found Orson Welles in the doorway in *The Third Man*.

Walker Percy
The Movie-goer, 1961

(*above*) Fred Zinnemann's *High Noon*; (*below*) Henry King's *The Gunfighter*

8

Introduction

This ruminative monograph is neither another defence of the Western nor a further attack upon it. My aim, I suppose, is to share with the sympathetic reader some of the reflections on the genre that I've had after thirty-odd years of movie-going. The brevity demanded by the format of the *Cinema One* series, and my resolve to concentrate upon areas where I feel I have something moderately original to say, have resulted in some fields of possible inquiry being ignored.

My concern here is entirely with American theatrical Westerns, mostly those made since 1950. The explanation for this decision is simple. First, I dislike TV horse operas (though a deal of what I say about screen Westerns applies to them too). Westerns need a large screen and are best enjoyed in the company of a thoughtful and occasionally noisy audience. Secondly, I cannot abide European Westerns, whether German, Italian or British, and I don't much like American Westerns filmed in Spain.* Thirdly, while many of my favourite

* There's a body of opinion which would argue that this disqualifies me as a true student of the genre. So be it. In fairness, therefore, I should direct the reader to the August 1970 double-issue of *Cinema* (numbers 6 and 7) which contains a concordance of the Italian Western by Mike Wallington and a study of the Italian Western by Chris Frayling. The July 1971 issue of *Films and Filming* has an article by David Austen on Continental Westerns and a filmography of 155 of them, which to me reads like a brochure for a season in hell.

pictures were made before the coming of sound, I have never cared for silent Westerns. Cowboy pictures need the pounding of hooves, the crack of Winchesters, the hiss of arrows, the stylised, laconic dialogue (which looks so terrible on paper, but is in fact the only consistently satisfactory period speech that the movies – or for that matter contemporary dramatic literature – have found), and the music, which if rightly used can give a picture the quality of a folk song. There are anyway several books – Fenin and Everson's, Charles Ford's, Jean-Louis Rieupeyrout's – which trace the genre's history from the turn-of-the-century to the 1960s, and combine with it a quantity of frontier history (in the case of Rieupeyrout's book, a great deal).

Partly through ignorance, partly through inclination, I do not belong to any particular school of criticism. Those versed in psychoanalysis could have, indeed have had, a field-day with the Western, but in considering the central significance of, say, gunplay, I am reminded of Freud's comment that 'sometimes a cigar is just a cigar'. There is, I am sure, a consistent Marxist interpretation of the Western, and I am aware that a good many structuralists currently find it fruitful to operate at a point where the apparatus of Lévi-Strauss and Company of Paris impinges upon the apparel of Levi Strauss and Co. of San Francisco. The reader will find little reflection of this here, nor will he be regaled with a Leavisian Great Tradition of the horse opera. My approach is largely a social, aesthetic and moral one.

For reasons of space, because I am dealing with general tendencies and characteristics of the genre and as there already exist numerous studies in French and English of single movies and the leading film-makers' œuvres, there are no detailed discussions here of individual pictures and directors. Moreover, some indifferent films may seem to have been mentioned or given disproportionate attention when far superior ones are ignored or scarcely touched on. So to indicate where I stand, let me say that I think the best Western ever made is the 1939 version of *Stagecoach*; that my favourite directors in the genre are John Ford (whose best movies perhaps are non-Westerns) and Anthony Mann (none of whose work outside the genre is particularly distinguished); and that, to show the catholicity and orthodoxy of my taste, my favourite twenty postwar Westerns (limiting myself to a single film per director) are, in chronological order: Howard Hawks' *Red River* (1948), John Ford's *Wagonmaster* (1950), Fred Zinnemann's *High Noon* (1952), George Stevens' *Shane* (1953), Robert Aldrich's *Vera Cruz* (1954), Charles Haas' *Star in the Dust* (1956), Samuel Fuller's *Run of the Arrow* (1956), Delmer Daves' *3.10 to Yuma* (1957), Anthony Mann's *Man of the West* (1958), John Sturges' *The Law and Jake Wade* (1958), Arthur Penn's *The Left-Handed Gun* (1958), Budd Boetticher's *Ride Lonesome* (1959), Don Siegel's *Flaming Star* (1960), Marlon Brando's *One Eyed Jacks* (1961), Sam Peckinpah's *Guns in the Afternoon* (1962), Gordon Douglas' *Rio Conchos* (1964), Henry Hathaway's *The Sons of Katie Elder* (1965), Martin Ritt's *Hombre* (1966), Robert Mulligan's *The Stalking Moon* (1968) and William Fraker's *Monte Walsh* (1970).

11

1: Politics, etc., and the Western

Hardly anyone alive can remember a time when there weren't Western movies. One of those who could was 'Broncho Billy' Anderson, star of Edwin S. Porter's *The Great Train Robbery* in 1903, and founder (with George Spoor) of the Essanay Company, pre-World War I specialists in cowboy pictures, and he died early in 1971 at the age of 88. Despite the temporary competition of gangster films, science fiction and spy movies, the Western continues to thrive, the subject of abuse, sometimes justified, sometimes not, but increasingly a matter for serious critical attention, some of it useful, some of it exceedingly heavy-handed.

There are two things that every schoolboy knows about the genre. First, that the Western is a commercial formula with rules as fixed and immutable as the Kabuki Theatre. Second, that the events depicted have little to do with the real nineteenth-century American frontier life, that the rituals are enacted in a timeless world where it is always high noon in some dusty cowtown west of St Louis. Rather like, in fact, the Never-Never Land of Barrie's *Peter Pan*, populated by children who refuse to grow up, fugitives from the urban nursery, marauding Indians and menacing bands of pirates.

Like most things that schoolboys so confidently know, neither of these simple contentions is wholly true, and there is general agreement that for better or worse the Western has changed significantly since World War II, becoming more varied, complex and self-conscious. We now have little difficulty in identifying the reasons for this change. There was the House Un-American Activities Committee's investigation of Hollywood in the Forties and Fifties, which caused the film industry to lose its nerve and look for safe subjects or a framework in which controversial issues could be handled in less obviously contentious fashion. There were the two generations which had passed since the official closing of the frontier by the US Census Bureau, two generations reared on cowboy pictures. Television gradually siphoned off the routine, B-feature Western, compelling the makers of movies for theatrical distribution to innovate. The introduction of widescreen processes in the early Fifties immediately benefited Western movies while initially posing problems for other subjects. The increasing availability of better, cheaper colour processes also favoured the Western. Then there was the steady decline of censorship until, with the replacement of the Hollywood production code by a series of guidelines in 1968, it virtually ceased to exist. All these factors have played their part.

In 1946 C. A. Lejeune in the *Observer* took the producers of *The Virginian* to task for attempting a more sophisticated approach to the genre: 'It is the greatest mistake to suppose that people want novelty in their cowboy pictures.' By 1950 Dilys Powell in the *Sunday Times* was able to write, with mild disapproval, of *The Gunfighter* as being made 'in the current intellectual, Western style'.

Of course there had been Westerns before which had dealt in a serious, responsible and often fairly complex way with adult themes, tragic situations and important aspects of the frontier experience. Such films were exceptional, however, and regarded as such, and very few of them can be viewed today without a good deal of indulgence. What I am talking about here is a major transformation which took place over a relatively short period, and which, in my view, revitalised the genre and opened

13

up new possibilities which might be described as boundless were it not that one recognises certain inherent limitations in the form.

In retrospect we can see those postwar years, which gave us John Ford's *My Darling Clementine* (1946) and his so-called cavalry trilogy (*Fort Apache, She Wore a Yellow Ribbon, Rio Grande*), King Vidor's *Duel in the Sun* (1948) and Howard Hawks' *Red River* (1948), as leading up to the watershed year of 1950 when, in a mere four months, Hollywood released Delmer Daves' first Western, *Broken Arrow*, Anthony Mann's first two cowboy movies, *Devil's Doorway* and *Winchester '73*, Ford's thoughtful *Wagonmaster* and Henry King's *The Gunfighter*. One French critic has even referred to 1950 as being 'a little like the 1789 of the genre's history'. Shortly after there came a stream of new-style Westerns, including the two immediately acclaimed instant 'classics', Fred Zinnemann's *High Noon* (1952) and George Stevens' *Shane* (1953), both by distinguished directors who were new to the genre and never returned to it.

In 1949 there was only a single important box-office star whose name was associated principally with the Western and that was John Wayne; and only a single major director, John Ford, and he had only directed five Westerns in the sound era, four of them starring Wayne. Up to the early Fifties there were separate industry polls for the 'Top Ten Box Office Stars' and the 'Top Ten Western Stars' (the latter reserved for low-budget performers), as if they were different sides of the business. All this was to change: Westerns began to attract the best acting talent, the most skilled writers and accomplished directors, not just for occasional forays but regularly and with decreasing condescension. Critical attitudes, however, did not change overnight. Individual Westerns marked by a manifest seriousness or an obvious contempt for the routine were admired or attacked less on their merits than according to the critics' view of what a Western should be. Meanwhile, in the English-

14

speaking world at least, the two most notable bodies of work from the Fifties – the Westerns of Anthony Mann and Budd Boetticher – went almost unnoticed, to be resurrected in the Sixties after Mann had turned his attention to epics and Boetticher had retired to Mexico to make a documentary about bull-fighting.

The sense of unease in the presence of the Western which still existed in the Fifties is well caught by Truman Capote in his *New Yorker* profile of Marlon Brando. Capote visited Brando in Kyoto, where he was filming *Sayonara*. Discussing his future, the star observed that

movies do have a great potential. You can say important things to a lot of people. I want to make pictures that explore the themes current in the world today. That's why I've started my own independent company.

Capote asked about the company's first picture, on the script of which Brando was then labouring.

And did *A Burst of Vermilion* satisfy him as a basis for the kind of lofty aims he proposed?

He mumbled something. Then he mumbled something else. Asked to speak more clearly, he said 'It's a Western.'

He was unable to restrain a smile, which expanded into laughter. He rolled on the floor and roared. 'Christ, the only thing is, will I ever be able to look my friends in the face again?' Sobering somewhat, he said, 'Seriously, though, the first picture *has* to make money. Otherwise there won't be another, I'm nearly broke . . .'

A little later Brando returned to the subject.

'But seriously though,' said Brando, now excessively sober, '*Burst* isn't just cowboys-and-Indians stuff. It's about this Mexican boy – hatred and discrimination. What happens to a community when these things exist.'*

---

* 'The Duke in His Domain', *Selected Writings of Truman Capote* (Hamish Hamilton, London, 1963), pp. 417–18.

One Eyed Jacks: 'a strong undertone of masochism'

A Burst of Vermilion eventually reached the screen some five years later as *One Eyed Jacks*, directed by Brando himself when Stanley Kubrick departed after a couple of days' shooting. The film was no laughing matter and Brando has less reason to be ashamed of it than he has for many of his pictures since *On the Waterfront*.

In 1961 *One Eyed Jacks* accorded with a new pattern which had developed in the Western. Some brooding, over-indulgent sequences, a strong undertone of masochism – these could be, and were, attributed to Brando's direction. But in viewing this study of the relationship between two former friends – one who retained his integrity as an outlaw, the other who revealed his weakness and hypocrisy through taking a job as lawman in a settled community – no one thought the elaborately detailed characterisation, the carefully worked out symbolism of cards and bullets, the loving creation of mood and the situating of people in the landscape, the atmosphere of dark pessimism or the suggestions of homosexuality, particularly new or remarkable. And anyway the film's considerable length was punctuated by set pieces – a bank robbery, two jail breaks and several gunfights – which were exemplarily staged enactments of familiar events.

Clearly a certain innocence had been lost: the children had got hold of Dr Spock and the nursery would never be the same again. A Catch-22 situation developed in which the charge of *faux-naïveté* could be brought against those who attempted to recapture a lost simplicity, while the too knowing or ambitious would be accused – not always unjustly – of being pretentious, decadent overreachers. Nevertheless, moviegoers and film-makers alike have continued to carry in their minds a firm notion of the archetypal Western where everything goes according to a series of happily anticipated moral and dramatic conventions – or clichés. Perhaps there was a time when this was so, though it is certainly no longer true. What created this feeling (and has sustained it) is the way in which Westerns good, bad and indifferent have always tended to coalesce in the memory into one vast, repetitious movie with a succession of muddled brawls in bar-rooms, tense and inscrutable poker games in smoky saloons, gunfights in empty streets, show-downs among the rocks with whining bullets, cavalry pursuits and Indian ambushes, mysterious strangers riding into town in search of vengeance or redemption, knights errant galloping to the relief of the oppressed. This simple image of the 'traditional Western' provides the movie-maker with a model upon which to ring variations and the audience with a yardstick by which to judge the latest product.

The late Frank Gruber, a prolific author of Western screen-plays and novels, is responsible for the widely quoted dictum that there are only seven basic Westerns: the railway story, the ranch story, the cattle empire story (which is the ranch story epically rendered), the revenge story, the cavalry versus Indians story, the outlaw story, and the marshal or 'law and order' story. While it is true that the vast majority of cowboy movies can be accommodated within these pigeon-holes, Gruber's Law would tell us little about the tone or character of any individual picture so deposited. For this reason a form of critical shorthand has grown up over the years which testifies to the problems writers have faced in indicating the kind of cowboy movie they are talking about. An incomplete list, which at least suggests some of the apparent variety within the genre, would include: 'Epic Western', 'Sur-Western' (or super-Western – a French coinage to describe large-scale works which betray the genre's essential simplicity), 'Adult Western', 'Satirical Western', 'Comedy Western', 'Chamber Western', 'Liberal Western', 'Sociological Western', 'Realistic Western', 'Anti-Western', 'Psychological Western', 'Allegorical Western' and, most recently, 'Spaghetti Western' (seized on by TV commercial makers to sell spaghetti hoops) and 'Paella Western'.

These are epithets to pin down the character of a movie. A further set of terms exists to locate, in time and space, action movies which resemble cowboy pictures but cannot strictly be regarded as Westerns. At one end of the time scale there is the 'pre-Western' which deals with the coonskin-capped frontiersman armed with a flintlock musket and travelling by foot in the late eighteenth–early nineteenth century, the Fenimore Cooper Leather-Stocking figure. At the end of the first half of *The Alamo* (1960), John Wayne as Davy Crockett abandons his coonskin cap and appears on the mission battlements wearing a black stetson to join his fellow heroes in a monumental grouping and stare out stoically at Santa Anna's Mexican force. The siege of the Alamo was in 1836, and marking as it does the death of two of the last legendary frontiersmen and the beginning of Texan independence from Mexico, we can regard this as a reasonable starting date for the genre, though in fact there are relatively few Westerns with pre-Civil War settings.

At the other end of the time scale is the 'Modern' or 'Post-Western', set in the present-day West where lawmen, rodeo

bove) *The Alamo:* coonskin caps on the battlements; (*below*) the Civil War *estern: The Long Ride Home* (George Hamilton, Inger Stevens)

riders and Cadillac-driving ranchers are still in thrall to t‍
frontier myth. Halfway between them is the Civil War movi‍
essentially the product of an established society; the Easter‍
terrain with its carefully cultivated land and lovingly tend‍
hedgerows, its Southern plantations, and a sun casting a mo‍
tolerant or seemingly benevolent light, creates an ambience,‍
psychological landscape quite alien to the Western proper.

The best Civil War pictures have been modestly conceive‍
productions situated in the margin of the conflict, whic‍
usually direct us away from the more divisive central issu‍
raised somewhat ambivalently in Michael Curtiz's *Santa* ‍
Trail (1940), which concludes with the hanging of John Brow‍
and most controversially by Griffith's *The Birth of a Natio*‍
One thinks of Ford's *The Horse Soldiers* (1959), Huston's *T*‍
Red Badge of Courage (1952), the Sanders Brothers' *Time O*‍
of War (1954), Hugo Fregonese's *The Raid* (1954; a supe‍
little movie about a group of escaped Southern POWs wh‍
infiltrate a Vermont town from Canada, which inspired Joh‍
Arden's *Serjeant Musgrave's Dance*), and Anthony Mann‍
The Tall Target (1952; a thriller concerning the frustration ‍
a plot to assassinate Lincoln on a Washington-bound train ‍
the eve of the war).

Several important Westerns have the Civil War as a bac‍
drop. A recurrent situation is the Western fort manned ‍
misfits and commanded by martinets who can be spared fro‍
the war (*The Last Frontier*, *Company of Cowards*), or t‍
conflict between Union soldiers and their Confedera‍
prisoners in Western outposts (*Two Flags West*, *Maj*‍
Dundee, *Escape from Fort Bravo*, and most uncompromising‍
The Long Ride Home, where unusually for this sub-species ‍
possibility of reconciliation is suggested). Equally a great nur‍
ber of Westerns, perhaps the majority, taking place in t‍
unceasing ripples of the war's aftermath, turn to the war as ‍
source of character definition and motivation: Southerne‍
drifting West to work as cowhands, ex-members of Colon‍

20

e notion that America was uniquely shaped by the frontier experience': John
rd's *Wagonmaster*

narles Quantrill's guerrilla band turning to civilian outlawry,
artime treacheries to be revenged (*The Deadly Companions*,
o Lobo) and so on. Tensions in the West on the eve of the
ivil War have attracted relatively few film-makers, though
leeding Kansas' is dealt with gingerly in *Santa Fé Trail* and
Melvin Frank's *The Jayhawkers* (a confused 1959 account
the Kansas insurrectionist movement).

Then there are the so-called 'Easterns', Japanese or Russian
ovies which resemble horse operas, and what are sometimes
lled 'para-Westerns' – tales of the Foreign Legion and
edieval knights which are cowboy pictures in different garb,
stories set in Australia or South Africa which attempt to
lebrate pioneer life there in a style clearly influenced by the
merican model.

The Western is not merely a cinematic form, but relates to a
uch larger international set of attitudes and beliefs, ranging
om the symbolic status conferred on 'the West' from the

21

dawn of civilisation, through everyone's ambivalent feeling about American culture, to the need for American politicians to define their public posture in relation to a national mythology. The notion that America was uniquely shaped by the frontier experience, though common currency for two centuries, was given its most eloquent and compelling form in the essays and speeches of the Wisconsin historian Frederic Jackson Turner, beginning with his celebrated 1893 address to the American Historical Association on 'The Significance of the Frontier in American Life'. The existence of an area of free land, its continual recession, and the advance of American settlement westward explain American development, Turner asserted. And he went on to claim that:

The result is that to the frontier the American intellect owes its striking characteristics. The coarseness and strength combined with acuteness and inquisitiveness; that practical, inventive turn of mind quick to find expedients; that masterful grasp of material things, lacking in the artistic but powerful to effect great ends; that restless nervous energy; that dominant individualism, working for good and for evil, and withal that buoyancy and exuberance which comes from freedom – these are the traits of the frontier or traits that are called out elsewhere because of the existence of the frontier.*

In highly charged language of a kind that has continued to be part of the obligatory rhetoric of America's politicians, though only rarely of her scholars, Turner put forward his heady thesis at the very time that the Western experience was coming to an end – three years after the Superintendent of the Census had announced that the frontier 'can not any longer have a place

---

* Reprinted in *Frontier and Section*, Selected Essays by Frederick Jackson Turner (Prentice-Hall, Spectrum Books, Englewood Cliffs, New Jersey, 1961), with introduction and notes by Turner's leading present-day follower Ray Allen Billington. There is an excellent account of Turner's life, ideas and influence in Richard Hofstadter's *The Progressive Historians* (Jonathan Cape, London, 1969).

e census reports', three years after the last desperate Indians for whose fate Turner's address evinced little regret – were massacred in the snow at Wounded Knee.

There is no theme you cannot examine in terms of the Western, no situation which cannot be transposed to the West, whether it be the Trojan War turned into a Texas range conflict Harry Brown's novel *The Stars in their Courses*, a pretentious work which has Philoctetes as Phil Tate, the ace gunslinger nursing an incurable wound down Mexico way, Odysseus as the rancher Oliver Swindon who heads out for the territory when the fighting is over, and so on) or *King Lear* as a prairie and baron (the late Anthony Mann's final, unrealised project). An talian company has made a frontier version of *Hamlet* (*Johnny Hamleto*), and Delmer Daves' *Jubal* (1956) appears to be based on *Othello*, with an Iago-like cowhand (Rod Steiger) arousing the jealousy of the ugly ranch boss (Ernest Borgnine) when the job of foreman goes to his younger rival (Glenn Ford).

The gangster movies *Kiss of Death* and *The Asphalt Jungle* become the cowboy pictures *The Fiend that Walked the West* and *The Badlanders*; the social melodrama *House of Strangers* (about a patriarchal Italian family in New York) becomes in *Broken Lance* a tale of a Texas rancher and his brood. Raoul Walsh's *Distant Drums* (1952) bears a striking resemblance to his war movie *Objective Burma* (1945), with Seminole Indians standing in for Japanese, boats for planes; rather more remotely, the William Holden Western vehicle *Alvarez Kelly* (1967) looks like an attempt to extract the salient dramatic and thematic qualities from Holden's biggest success *The Bridge on the River Kwai* and relocate them in the American Civil War. A child could tell (and indeed a TV-watching child did tell me) that Kurt Neumann's *Cattle Drive* (1951) is virtually a dry-land version of Kipling's *Captains Courageous*, with Joel McCrea as a trail boss taming the spoilt upper-class brat Dean Stockwell, just as earlier Spencer Tracy's Grand Banks fisherman had performed a similar service for Freddie Bartholomew.

Akira Kurosawa's two greatest international successe:
Rashomon and *The Seven Samurai*, were both bought up b
Hollywood as the basis for the Westerns *The Outrage* (1964) an
The Magnificent Seven (1960), while his later *Yojimbo*, whic
Kurosawa admits was influenced by *High Noon* and *Shane*, wa
plagiarised for the first Spaghetti Western to receive wid
international distribution, Sergio Leone's *A Fistful of Dollars*

The Western is a great grab-bag, a hungry cuckoo of
genre, a voracious bastard of a form, open equally to visior
aries and opportunists, ready to seize anything that's in the a:
from juvenile delinquency to ecology. Yet despite this, or i
some ways because of it, one of the things the Western :
always about is America rewriting and reinterpreting her ow
past, however honestly or dishonestly it may be done. Th
inadequacy of the Western is less my immediate concern her
than its power or persuasiveness. Take any subject and drop i
down west of the Mississippi, south of the 49th Parallel an
north of the Rio Grande between 1840 and World War :
throw in the mandatory quantity of violent incidents, and yo
have not only a viable commercial product but a new an
disarmingly fresh perspective on it. Such at least is the hop
and intention.

Consequently I would like to propose a way of looking at th
Western over the past twenty years through a series of simpl
categories which recognises the diverse factors working upo:
it. The system depends upon making connections between th
style, tone and content of movies and the rhetoric, beliefs an
public personae of four prominent politicians. So it might b
useful to preface my thesis by pointing to the associatio:
between two American artists and a leading statesman whic:
throws some light on this question.

They were the three Ivy League friends, the Yale Art Schoo
drop-out Frederic Remington, the Harvard graduate Theodor:
Roosevelt and the other Harvard alumnus, Owen Wister. The:
were all well-born Easterners who went West in the late nine

eenth century — Wister for his health and Roosevelt and Remington as ranchers, an activity at which both failed. Having tasted the painful reality of prairie life, they proceeded to help shape the visual, ideological and literary myth of the West which has come down to us. In doing so the trio can be regarded as having exerted an influence quite as powerful as the dime novels and stage melodramas from which the Western movie sprang at the turn of the century. Because people took their words and images seriously.

A painter and sculptor, Remington became the most popular non-photographic recorder of the vanishing West as well as a notable illustrator and war correspondent; his work adorned Lyndon Johnson's White House and he has influenced the visual style of numerous 'realistic' Westerns of recent years — his paintings are used behind the credit titles of Richard Brooks' *The Last Hunt* (1956), and whole sequences of *The Culpepper Cattle Company* (1972) and *Monte Walsh* (1970) look like animated Remingtons. The latter has credit titles based on paintings by another closely associated Western artist, Charles B. Russell.* When Peter Bogdanovich† asked John Ford, 'Which of your cavalry pictures are you most pleased with?' the director replied:

---

* There is a stimulating article, 'Painters of the Purple Sage', by Harris Rosenstein in *Art News* (Summer, 1968) on the association of Remington, Wister and Roosevelt. Reviewing an exhibition of work by Remington and Russell called 'How the West Was Won', Rosenstein takes a fairly charitable view of the latter and a very scathing one of the former:

There is . . . about Remington, most especially in his deadpan skillfulness, and aura of depressive guilty knowledge, the sense of an inner life not bottled up but atrophied by involvements that looked real but never were. In a way, cinematic virtuosity in the Western owes something to Remington in that by such ultimately irrelevant commitments as he had, he managed to dehumanise and sterilise the iconography. What he does is to kill the man but leave the dapperness, and with dapper dummies we have the props for a ventriloqual act.

† *John Ford* (Studio Vista, London, 1967), p. 87.

25

I like *She Wore a Yellow Ribbon*. I tried to copy the Remington style there – you can't copy him one hundred per cent – but at least I tried to get his colour and movement, and I think I succeeded partly.

The politician-adventurer Theodore Roosevelt was within the American tradition of the intellectual as man-of-action. He wrote widely and romantically of life on the plains, produced a four-volume, White Anglo-Saxon Protestant interpretation of America's continental expansion, *The Winning of the West*, became a military hero, President of the United States, and played a significant part in taking America into World War I.

With *The Virginian*, Owen Wister, literary protégé of Henry James, rose above the dime novel fiction of the day and wrote what is, for all its shortcomings, the first major Western novel. It was illustrated by Remington in one edition, by Charles Russell in another, and dedicated to Roosevelt on first publication in 1902; in 1911 it was rededicated 'to the greatest benefactor we people have known since Lincoln', in a prefatory note which hits out at both Wall Street and the emergent trade unions.

The best-known phrase from *The Virginian* – now a Western cliché but one which long preceded the coming of sound – is the hero's tight-lipped, 'When you call me that – smile.' The fictional provenance of the phrase is less well known and worth noting. Early in the book, the Virginian is called a son-of-a-bitch (though Wister cannot bring himself to write the term) and takes it in good part as an affectionate remark by a friend. Later, during a poker game, the villainous Trampas uses the same words, but this time the Virginian, as becomes an eminent Victorian, is not amused. The naive Eastern narrator observes:

Something had been added to my knowledge also. Once again I had heard applied to the Virginian that epithet that Steve so freely used. The same words, identical to the letter. But this time they had

26

The Remington style: (*above*) *The Culpepper Cattle Company*; (*below*) *Monte Walsh*

produced a pistol. 'When you call me that, *smile!*' So I perceived a new example of the letter that means nothing until the spirit gives it life.

My thesis turns on the names of four numinous figures who emerged in the early Fifties. The first pair are John F. Kennedy and Barry Goldwater, respectively the spokesmen for the New Frontier and the Old Frontier, who were both freshman senators in 1953. The second pair are Lyndon Johnson, who became Senate majority leader during President Eisenhower's first term, and William Buckley, whose *God and Man at Yale* and *McCarthy and his Enemies* established him in the same period as the most articulate representative of the New Conservatism.

In the 1964 Presidential Election America was faced with a choice between two self-conscious Westerners, both sons of pioneer familes – Johnson from Texas and Goldwater from Arizona. One was a Democrat who originally entered politics in the Populist tradition which his political grandfather and father adhered to (though his own career was to take him ever further away from this, with tragic results); the other is a right-wing Republican and proponent of rugged individualism. Campaigning for office, Johnson claimed that he would avoid the rash, violent courses of action which Goldwater's foreign policy threatened. A sadly depopulated Texas township is named after one of Johnson's forbears and a rather grand ranch carries his initials or brand; several Arizona department stores bear the anglicised name of Goldwater's grandfather. The Easterners, Kennedy and Buckley, were both educated at Ivy League universities, came from rich Catholic families dominated by determined patriarchs, and gained an early reputation for style and wit; one was a liberal Democrat, the other is an extreme Conservative. Kennedy made his 1960 ticket secure by taking on LBJ as his vice-presidential running partner to get the Southern and South-Western vote. Buckley

28

once conducted an elegant losing campaign in 1965 for Mayor of New York against the progressive John Lindsay, and when asked what he would do if he were elected, answered quick as a flash, 'I'd demand a recount.'

The principal stylistic features of a typical Kennedy Western might be defined thus: the overall treatment would be taut and fast-driving; its rhetoric would be elegant, ironic, laced with wit; pictorially the images would be carefully composed, bringing out the harsh challenge of the landscape; its moral tone would be sharp and penetrating; its mood would be cool with an underlying note of the absurd or tragic sense of life; the past would be rendered in a moderately realistic fashion, almost without regret, just a token elegiacism. The overall style of the typical Goldwater Western would be slack and expansive; its rhetoric would be sententious, broadly humorous, woolly; its visual surface would involve a casual acceptance of the landscape; the moral tone would be generous but ultimately unforgiving, riding on a knife-edge between cruelty and sentimentality; its mood would be warmly nostalgic.

The content of the Kennedy Western would tend to feature the following ingredients: a slightly diffident hero, capable of change and development, with a rather unostentatious professionalism, though prone to a sense of anguished failure; there would be an accent on the need for community activity; minorities and aliens would be viewed sympathetically, compassionately; opposition would be expressed to the notion that man is essentially or necessarily violent; there would be an implication that one should look to the past for guidance towards the creation of a new and better condition in the future; the underlying argument would favour a wry optimism about the future development of society.

The content of the Goldwater Western on the other hand, in its extreme form, would tend to reflect almost the opposite of these elements: the hero would be resolute, unswerving, rock-like in his own virtue and image of himself; emphasis would fall on individualism, self-help, the inevitability of inequality; it would see aggression as a natural aspect of man, and violence as unavoidable and perhaps to be enjoyed, certainly to be anticipated; a suspicious or somewhat patronising attitude would be shown to aliens and minorities; the general feeling would be that one should look to the past to find an ideal of behaviour and to discover how society should be organised; the underlying emphasis would support a guarded pessimism with an opposition to change unless it meant a possibility of moving back and regaining a golden age in the past.

The interplay between the Kennedy content and the Kennedy style produces the Kennedy Western; similarly for the Goldwater Western. However, if you treat the Kennedy content with the Goldwater style you get the Johnson Western, and if you apply the Kennedy style to the Goldwater content you get the Buckley Western. Inevitably, style transforms content and content modifies style, and this indeed is part of my argument; one corollary of which is that a film-maker is more likely to swing between Goldwater and Johnson Westerns or between Kennedy and Buckley movies than between the alternative pairings, despite the obvious ideological affinities.

Thus John Ford's Westerns since the late 1940s fall into the Goldwater or Johnson categories: *The Searchers* (1956) is clearly a Goldwater picture, while *Two Rode Together* (1961), which is virtually a reprise of the same subject (two men looking for pioneers captured by Indians), is probably a Johnson Western, as more obviously is the later *Cheyenne Autumn* (1964). All of Anthony Mann's films of the Fifties are Kennedy Westerns (except for his final masterpiece *Man of the West*, written by the liberal television playwright Reginald Rose: a real Buckley movie, whereas Mann's Kennedy films were scripted by the ultra-right wing Borden Chase). So are Delmer Daves'; but Budd Boetticher's films, with their close stylistic affinities, are Buckley movies. A striking example of a McCarthy period Buckley Western would be Charles Marquis

Warren's *Arrowhead* of 1953. (See my later sections on Indians.)

On another level, one would note that John Wayne's *The Alamo* (1960) was a Goldwater Western which, under the guise of saying 'better Tex than Mex' in its account of the first tragic stage in the winning of Texas from the Mexicans, was actually affirming 'better dead than Red', with rhetorical material about the Republic of Texas (as opposed to American democracy) seemingly drawn from the Blue Book of the John Birch Society. But *The Alamo* was a Goldwater Western at the time when the junior senator from Arizona was in the wilderness. In 1964, when Goldwater was shaping up as the Republican Party's presidential candidate, Wayne came out with *McClintock!*, a carefully guarded defence of middle-American Goldwaterism. Setting aside the coonskin cap of Davy Crockett and the blood and steel of *The Alamo*, Wayne now appeared as a benevolent turn-of-the-century New Mexico cattle baron with the appropriate name of George Washington McClintock. He happily embraces hard-working poor whites, bureaucrat-harassed Indians, mid-Western university graduates and a Jewish storekeeper (numbered among his close friends and admirers, and clearly reminiscent to 1964 audiences of Goldwater's grandfather, 'Big Mike' Goldwasser) as equal partners in the free-enterprise, self-help system. On the other side are the butts of the movie's unconcealed animus and heavy-handed comedy — Eastern dilettantes, the unappreciative young (an Ivy League college boy even apologises to Wayne for calling him a reactionary!), government agents, do-gooders and everyone else who has since earned the alliterative animosity and sarcastic scorn of Spiro Agnew. This 'silent majority' Western might be taken as an anticipation of the emergence of the former governor of Maryland on to the national scene in 1968 and into this scheme.

I worked out these loose categories in 1963. Since the death of John Kennedy they have become less clear-cut, though I

believe they remain equally valid and more interesting. Wit
the sympathy for Black Panthers at home and revolutionar
movements abroad which has been growing on the left, and th
support for the Vietnam war and 'law'n'order' on the righ
America's orientation towards violence has reverted to mor
primitive patterns, while at the same time political lines hav
become confused in the centre, sharper on the fringes.

One can see the blurring of the lines in the career of Sar
Peckinpah, whose social ideas and political attitudes are bot
more complex and less clearly articulated than Wayne's. Peck
inpah made his name in 1962 with *Guns in the Afternoon* (a
Ride the High Country was called in Britain), a Kenned
Western in which a pair of ageing marshals realise that thei
world is coming to an end and prepare two youngsters for
transformed society. He ended the decade with *The Wil
Bunch* (1969), a violent, apocalyptic movie which back in th
early Sixties would have been an obvious Buckley Western – i
contrast to *The Magnificent Seven* (1960), where a les
equivocal wild bunch intervene in the internal politics c
Mexico almost as if they had anticipated the call of Kennedy'
inaugural address. The difference is analogous to that betwee
two creations of John Kennedy – the Peace Corps and th
Green Berets. Now one views *The Wild Bunch* as a new-style
soured Kennedy Western and a rather obvious and bitte
allegory about Vietnam, and one observes that the bunch'
leader bears the name 'Pike Bishop', which may or may not b
a conscious reference to that key figure of the America
Sixties, California's late Bishop James Pike, humanist mysti
and ecclesiastical drop-out.

Another late Sixties variant of the Kennedy Western i
Butch Cassidy and the Sundance Kid (1969), which enjoyed
popularity similar to that of *The Magnificent Seven* ten year
earlier. With its cute, knowing style borrowed from fashio
magazines, Sunday supplements and Pop Art, its cultivation c
the insouciant, anti-social hero who goes off to fight his fina

'Radical chic': *Butch Cassidy and the Sundance Kid*; and (*below*): 'a new-style, ~~c~~oured Kennedy Western': American intervention in *The Wild Bunch*

33

High Noon: star in the dust

battles in the Bolivian mountains after the manner of Che Guevara, *Butch Cassidy* is a prime example of what Tom Wolfe has called 'radical chic'.

As an illustration of the way American life throws light on the Western and the Western illuminates American life, one could do no better than point to what ten years ago appeared to be the archetypal Kennedy and Goldwater Westerns – the Kennedy *High Noon* (1952) and the Goldwater *Rio Bravo* (1959). The latter, expressly made by Howard Hawks as a riposte to Fred Zinnemann's *High Noon*, features John Wayne as a sheriff doing precisely the opposite of what Gary Cooper did in the earlier picture: he never for a moment loses his cool or doubts himself; instead of going round soliciting aid from reluctant townsfolk, he actually turns down the offer of help from non-professionals. And as we know, Wayne was incensed by what he thought was a leftist plot to betray Cooper and was particularly offended by the parting shot of the Zinnemann picture when Cooper throws his badge of office in the dust

34

High Noon was carefully blue-printed before shooting and lasts an intense 84 minutes (roughly the time of the action); *Rio Bravo* was written as it went along and rambles on for around two and a half hours. Today, in the Seventies, these two pictures can be interpreted in a rather different fashion.

High Noon, initially an allegory about existential man standing alone in the McCarthy era (and scripted as his last Hollywood picture by a McCarthy victim, Carl Foreman), now suggests an over-commitment to an abstract principle. Marshal Kane could have cleared out of town and escaped the four gunmen who were coming to get him when the noon train arrived. He had after all retired with all his previous obligations fulfilled. I still find *High Noon* moving, intelligent and gripping, but I am no longer able to accept it as the splendidly liberal statement which it seemed to so many of us in the Fifties; and I am less inclined to laugh at the interpretation made at that time by the Swedish critics who found in it a quite different 'politisk-allegorisk dubbelmening'. Both Gunnar Oldin,* in an analysis of Stanley Kramer's early productions, and Harry Schein, in his essay *The Olympian Cowboy*,* read *High Noon* as an allegory about American foreign policy and the Korean War. The marshal (America) had wanted peace after clearing up the town five years before (i.e., World War II), and reluctantly must buckle on his gunbelt again in the face of new aggression (the Korean War), and eventually his pacifist wife (American isolationists) must see where her true duty lies and support him. 'The sum total,' wrote Schein, 'seems to be that of course pacifism can be a good thing but that war in certain given circumstances may be both moral and inevitable.' Given this interpretation, John Wayne might well have leapt at the opportunity to make a contemporary Vietnam version of *High Noon* which reflected

* Oldin's 'En amerikansk tragedi' and Schein's 'Den olympiske cowboyen' are in *Skott I Mörkret* (Wahlström & Widstrand, Stockholm, 1956); Schein's essay is translated in *The American Scholar* (Summer, 1955).

Julie Nixon Eisenhower's claim during the 1972 Presidential Campaign that she would be 'willing to die for the Thieu regime'.

Compared with the earlier picture, *Rio Bravo*, in which Wayne actually has a prisoner in the jailhouse to hold for a mere couple of days – an expressly limited commitment, essentially defensive in character – seems to rest on a more solid foundation. There is of course a totally different tone to each of these films which – and this is my point – makes it necessary to consult the prevailing political climate at the time they were made to reveal their conscious meanings. However, the inbuilt ironies and contradictions of the Kennedy Western *and* of John Kennedy's political postures are to be found in *High Noon*. In a highly diverting documentary play called *John Ford's Cuban Missile Crisis* which Albert Hunt and his students at the Bradford College of Art produced a couple of years ago, the 1962 Kennedy–Khruschev confrontation over Cuba was presented as a Western directed by John Ford in which the American president was seen as a Henry Fonda figure, talking like a dove and acting like a hawk.

Further thought perhaps must be given to Richard Nixon's position in this framework. For, as we know, that impressionable moviegoer saw *Patton* the night before he sanctioned the invasion of Cambodia and had a private screening of John Wayne in *Chisum* the evening before addressing the American Bar Association conference in Denver, when he coyly expatiated on the perennial appeal of the Western ('This may be a square observation,' but 'the good guys come out ahead and the bad guys lose') and embarrassingly prejudged the then *sub judice* Manson trial. At the 1972 Republican Party Convention at Miami, John Wayne returned the compliment by presenting a series of film clips from the President's career, while James Stewart did the same for Mrs Nixon.*

---

* Since completing this book I am happy to discover that Eric Bentley has been thinking along similar lines. His Theatre of War (Eyre Metheun,

Nixon's interest in the genre is oddly enough paralleled by Joseph Stalin's, as vouchsafed to us in *Kruschev Remembers*, where we read that for film shows at the Kremlin Stalin

> used to select the movies himself. The films were usually what you might call captured trophies: we got them from the West. Many of them were American pictures. He liked cowboy movies especially. He used to curse them and give them the proper ideological evaluation but then immediately order new ones.*

Cursing horse operas, giving them the proper ideological evaluation and then immediately ordering new ones – Stalin sounds like the universal Western fan and critic. What a pity it was that this highly critical student of the genre never got an opportunity to see *Storm in the West*.† This was an interpretation of the events leading up to World War II written by Sinclair Lewis and Dore Schary in 1943 in the form of an allegorical, didactic Western. Stalin figured in it as Joel Slavin, a Civil War veteran from Georgia (where else?) who takes over 'the old Nicholas place' and later joins Ulysses Saunders (America) and Walter Chancel (Churchill) in a popular front against the outlaws Hygatt, Gribble, Gerrett and Mullison, whose iniquities have included gunning down Chuck Slattery (Czechoslovakia). Fred Zinnemann was among the directors

---

London, 1973) contains an essay called 'The Political Theatre of John Wayne' in which he observes:

> The most important American of our time is John Wayne. Granted that all good things come from California, Richard Nixon and Ronald Reagan are only camp followers of Wayne, supporting players in the biggest Western of them all, wagons hitched to Wayne's star. In an age when the image is the principal thing, Wayne is the principal image, and if the soul of this image is *machismo* (a topic for another essay, a topic for a book, for *the* book of our time), its body is the body politic, and its name is Anti-Communism.

* Trans. Strobe Talbott (André Deutsch, London, 1971), p. 297.

† The screenplay, rendered in narrative form with Sol Baer Fielding's pre-production illustrations and an introduction by Dore Schary, was published twenty years later (Stein and Day, New York, 1963; Sidgwick and Jackson, London, 1964).

considered for the weighty undertaking, but the script was rejected by the reigning MGM moguls as being 'too political'. One of their objections was to a close-up of a hammer and sickle hanging on the back of Joel Slavin's covered wagon.

Dore Schary attached such importance to *Storm in the West* that he resigned from MGM when the project was aborted. Sinclair Lewis, on the other hand, as his biographer Mark Schorer has suggested, was intrigued but rather less than totally committed. 'I still can't take the movies seriously,' he wrote to a friend. Yet in the mid-Thirties Lewis had written an unsuccessful play with a Western theme, *Jayhawker* (the first major professional production to be directed by Joseph Losey), in which the activities of the then threatening 'native fascism' of Louisiana's Governor Huey Long were rendered in allegorical form as a drama about the Kansas insurrectionist movement. At the very least Lewis was engaged by the virtuoso aspects of the film – the resonant names, the sharp parallels of plot, and so on. Oddly enough – or perhaps not so oddly – George Orwell was working on a quite different kind of allegory on the same subject which also led to publication problems. Orwell's embattled, over-explicit preface to *Animal Farm* has only recently come to light and, had it accompanied his book, would clearly have changed our feelings about the novel and probably have limited its appeal and shortened its life. Schary wrote a reminder to himself aimed to keep the allegory on the tracks and the movie on the MGM conveyor belt:

The one big point behind the entire production must be the fact that no one connected with it should be concerned too much with the symbols that they stand for. They must be concerned with the people and the characters that have been created for them. The direction must be related to a western motion picture, not a picture of significance. The whole thing must be done so that when it is finished and shown, a person who had never heard of Hitler and the second world war could look at it and enjoy it for what it is.

It was as natural perhaps for Orwell to have gone to English rural life as it was for Schary to have resorted to the Western for their allegorical exercises. *Storm in the West* was never made and consequently we are unable to judge its effects; *Animal Farm* is now a classic work of allegorical satire that wholly transcends the immediate conditions which produced it.

In the terminology of William Empson, both *Animal Farm* and *Storm in the West* are 'versions of Pastoral', a traditional source of allegory. Orwell went on to a different form and produced the science fiction novel *1984*. (So did Dore Schary with his appalling *The Next Voice You Hear* in 1949.) Science fiction and the Western are at once complementary and antithetical forms. Both are concerned with teaching lessons to the present through a rewriting of the past or by extrapolations of current tendencies projected into the future. Science fiction, however, is able to create a new consciousness – its realm is that of ideas, of apocalypse, and can treat of population growth, mutants, time, galactic travel, theology, mental telepathy, etc. The Western is earthbound and circumscribed; its province is the simpler, traditional concerns of man, where moral problems are considered by locating them in a pared-down historical framework. The ultimate root of the Western is man and the traditional concerns of character and community; science fiction at best involves the free play of intellect in a self-defining milieu where anything is possible and the terrain infinitely pliable.

Horace Gregory, in a masterly attack on the limitations and deceptions of the Western cult, concluded by suggesting that the Western was doomed to give way to science fiction:

It is probable that the cowboy cult will dwindle in favour of another plastic, easily malleable symbol of American hopes, hilarities and fears, and within another decade the noise of jet-propelled space

rockets on TV sets will drown out, tune out the explosions soundi
from the guns of the roaring West.*

Gregory has been proved wrong; and so has the German se
Robert Junck, who at the same time claimed to have seen t
moment when young American TV audiences abandoned t
West and Hopalong Cassidy in favour of galactic exploratio

I saw the downfall of Hoppy and the rise of his rival foreshadow
on the evening I had to dine with my Boston hosts without t
presence of Johnnie. To his father's astonishment the hoste
returned from the living room, from which emerged the sound
Hoppy's gallop, not alone as we had expected, but accompanied t
her offspring, a pale little boy who remarked by way of explanatio
'That guy is beginning to bore me.'
    A month later his father had bought him a space suit ($24.50), a
antidote against cosmic rays (sweets at 60 cents) and a pair of ant
gravity shoes ($7.20).†

Such has not come to pass – maybe science fiction becan
science fact sooner than Gregory and Junck foresaw. Anywa
Marshall McLuhan in *The Medium is the Massage* chose t
present a silhouette of a stagecoach in a driving mirror as
double-page spread to illustrate his contention that

The past went that-a-way. When faced with a totally new situatio
we tend always to attach ourselves to the objects, to the flavor of t
most recent past. We look at the present through a rear-view mirro
We march backwards into the future. Suburbia lives imaginatively i
Bonanza-land.‡

    I have invoked *Animal Farm* not only because of the c
incidence of its composition with that of *Storm in the West*, b

---

* 'Guns of the Roaring West', *Avon Book of Modern Writing No.*
(Avon Publications, New York, 1954).
    † *Tomorrow is Already Here* (Rupert Hart-Davis, London, 1954),
212.
    ‡ Allen Lane, The Penguin Press, London, 1967, p. 73.

lso because it raises the whole question of allegory in our ime. We don't read *Animal Farm* to understand the nature of otalitarian politics; it isn't an imaginative footnote which lluminates Orwell's life and thought or his sizeable body of political writing, which is undeniably more complex and far-eaching than this 120-page book. *Animal Farm* exists in its wn right, independent of its easily definable political proven-nce, in the way that all great satire does from Aristophanes hrough Dean Swift. By analogy and with certain reservations, he same is true of the Western movie. Unlike *Animal Farm* nd *Gulliver's Travels*, however, the film-maker is drawing on body of established knowledge readily accessible to the udience – in the same way, though for different reasons, that playwrights in, say, German-occupied France of World War II esorted to themes from classical mythology, or Eastern 'uropean dramatists and movie directors have reworked istorical subjects or used Aesopian language in handling mbiguous contemporary fables. An immediate judgment, ften rendered between the lines rather than explicitly, might cknowledge the dangerousness and present value of the enter-rise, and this can be as true of Hollywood as of Hungary. But n enduring response and ultimate judgment will inevitably be ased on less ephemeral criteria.

In proposing my categories of the Kennedy, Goldwater, ohnson and Buckley Western, therefore, I am not attempting o establish any hierarchy of values but rather to suggest a link etween contemporary pressures of various kinds and an exist-ng body of material which is constantly subjected to them. In he long run – when, as Keynes observed, we are all dead – here are no prizes for daring or innovation. It depends of ourse on whether we are making aesthetic judgments or min-ng popular culture for its sociological value, the latter being a ascinating if rather dangerous enterprise. *High Noon* touched ff a series of law'n'order Westerns, and only the movie histor-an will be aware that it did so; and two of them – *Star in the*

41

Dust and *Rio Bravo* – were clearly superior to the origina
Likewise with *Winchester '73*, the commercial success o
which inspired a cycle of 'weapon-Westerns' – *Colt 4.
Springfield Rifle*, *The Battle at Apache Pass* – none of ther
equalling the original; and only a social historian bent o
arguing from effect to cause would claim that they answered a
existing public need. Indeed the ingenious and persuasiv
Lawrence Alloway has so argued, and in defining the subjec
matter of the cycle as being 'not only about the power ne
weapons gave their owners, but about the social impact an
consequences of new weapons,' suggests (if I understand hi
rightly) that these Westerns expressed the prevailing ethos o
the pre- and early Eisenhower years which focused on equality
on closing the gap, in the Cold War arms race; and in the lat
Fifties, anticipating the advent of Kennedy, 'interest shifted t
operational lore and responsibility (*Gunman's Walk*, *The Ti
Star*, *The Young Guns*, *Saddle the Wind*): another cycle.'*

The most notable cycle at the time of writing is that inspire
by Peckinpah's *The Wild Bunch* (1969), a series of imitativ
and mostly grossly inferior pictures including Don Medford
The Hunting Party (1971), Daniel Mann's *The Revenger
(1972), Michael Winner's *Chato's Land* (1972) and Joh
Sturges' *Joe Kidd* (1972), all of which focus upon a disparat
band of utterly corrupt hunters accompanied (or led) by som
fairly decent character who is increasingly sickened by h
companions and the task in hand. These pursuers have th
support, more or less, of society and the law; their quarries a
outlaws but generally sympathetic ones, possessed of greate
character and moral strength than their trackers. Th
immediate political and allegorical background to thes
ferociously brutal stories is almost certainly the conditions o
the Vietnam war and the moral confusion that conflict ha
engendered. At a social level the movies are reflecting currer

* 'Iconography of the Movies': *Movie*, No. 7 (London, 1963).

ncerns and anxieties; from a commercial point of view a ofitable subject is being exploited that seems to go down well the box-office; viewed aesthetically, the cycle of movies is fering a cumulative series of variations upon an established eme.

Westerns don't appear to date like most movies, though I ncy I could see a ten-minute sequence of any cowboy picture d place it within a year of its production and probably – such the enduring tradition of studio styles and laboratory process- g – assign it to the right studio. The real judgments are sthetic, and as a result even Marxists and the Structuralist itics finish up celebrating the Westerns of Howard Hawks, hn Ford and Samuel Fuller and rejecting (or denouncing) eral Westerns such as *High Noon* or William Wyler's United ations hymn to peaceful coexistence, *The Big Country*. This, feel, is fair enough, though having lived through these years d being by inclination a social historian I necessarily view y movie both in its immediate context and *sub specie aeter- tatis*.

This leads me on to three cardinal aspects of the Western hich I can only deal with briefly.

First, the Western is ill-equipped to confront complex olitical ideas in a direct fashion. The genre belongs to the merican populist tradition which sees all politics and oliticians as corrupt and fraudulent – the political career of mes Stewart in *The Man Who Shot Liberty Valance* (1961) treated by Ford as pure burlesque (totally lacking the armth he brought to corrupt Boston politics in *The Last urrah*); the local politicians in Don Siegel's *Death of a unfighter* and Burt Kennedy's *The Good Guys and the Bad uys* are ludicrous caricatures, fantasy figures denied any imanity. One has to admit that the genre apparently cannot ccommodate the problems of on-going political life and the mpromises it involves. The 'Free Silver' issue, for instance, as one of the major concerns of frontier history and the

(*left*) *Terror in a Texas Town*; (*right*) *My Darling Clementine*: Wyatt Earp (He
Fonda) among the giant Saguaro cacti

Populist Movement, but not surprisingly it is a hopeless
complex matter ignored by the Western, except for *Silver Ri*
(1947). Raoul Walsh's film begins interestingly and in suitab
symbolic fashion with Errol Flynn being disgraced for destro
ing the paper money cargo of a Union Army payroll wagon
prevent it from falling into Confederate hands on the last day
the Civil War, and then sends him out West to become rath
tediously involved in silver mining and the obscure politics
the gold and silver controversy.

Secondly, the Western is an occasion for various kinds
virtuosity, a much disparaged quality at the present time whi
I am inclined to view as a disinterested, self-justifying ente
prise. Admirers of Sergio Leone see his four Westerns and o
Post-Western (*Giù la Testa*, 1971) in this way, as a kind
opera; less indulgently, I recognise odd individual sequenc
which stage a gunfight or a cattle drive in an interesting ma
ner, or certain movies such as Monte Hellman's *The Shooti*

hich employ the conventions of the genre in a bizarre and dividual way, as enlarging the vocabulary of the Western. evertheless one must be cautious – virtuosity is not the same ; creative imagination (Ford, for example, was continually xtending his range while rarely indulging in obtrusive bravura equences), and must be distinguished from gimmickry. Sterlg Hayden as a Scandinavian seaman going down main street meet his adversaries equipped with a lethal harpoon was a mple one-off, unrepeatable encounter in Joseph H. Lewis' *error in a Texas Town* (1958). At a very different level, the nal showdown in Hawks' *Red River*, where no one was killed d a sort of reason prevailed, could not establish a new onvention although it responded to the demands of a *bienensant* element of the audience; it was effective precisely ecause it worked against the true wishes of the spectators.

The form of virtuosity which has traditionally aroused the e of many dedicated Western fans has been what they conder the indulgent cultivation of the merely picturesque. In a 964 review of Walsh's *A Distant Trumpet* in the *Observer*, ingsley Amis complained of the way in which directors, stead of getting on with the action, allowed the camera to nger on the texture of Indians' head-dresses, just as ten years efore Robert Warshow had deplored the 'unhappy preccupation with style' in Ford's *Stagecoach* and the same estheticising tendency' in *My Darling Clementine*, though he und the latter 'a soft and beautiful movie'. Having been to Ionument Valley, where Ford shot *Clementine*, I now ppreciate that it is nothing like Tombstone and, more importntly, that there are no giant Saguaro cacti in that part of rizona. Consequently, in whatever scene this species of cactus gures as a component of an impressive composition, it must ave been placed there by Ford and his designer. This is most riking in the opening party at the still uncompleted church, here Henry Fonda and Cathy Downs tentatively move toards each other across the floor and three saguaros stand in

the background between them at the poignant moment whe
they look into each other's eyes and then start to dance.

As I say elsewhere in this book, I am as happy to see
camera play over the seductive Western landscape as I a
being regaled with the destruction of a saloon bar. The terra
and the décor are as worthy of detailed contemplation as tl
fortunes of those who inhabit and exhibit them. In the Weste
the *trompe l'œil* tradition of nineteenth-century American art
wedded to the landscape painting tradition. A striking case
point is the conclusion of Robert Parrish's remarkable *T*
Wonderful Country (1959), so beautifully photographed k
Floyd Crosby. Scripted, appositely some might think, k
Robert Ardrey, subsequently to be celebrated as the author
The Territorial Imperative, the film centres on the quest for
national identity of one Martin Brady (Robert Mitchum),
man troubled by the same problems of allegiance as his fello
Irish-Americans, O'Meara (Rod Steiger) in Fuller's *Run of tl*
Arrow and Captain Benjamin Tyreen (Richard Harris)
Peckinpah's *Major Dundee*.

When we first see Brady he is almost a parody of a Mexica
as he rides lethargically through a Texas border town clad
sombrero and poncho, oblivious to the dust-storm blowir
around him, on the handsome black horse presented to him k
his Mexican war-lord employer and called, suitabl
'Lacrimas'. After the complex events through which he move
in Texas and Mexico, he emerges at the end in an early mor
ing mist on the Southern bank of the Rio Grande. An assass
shoots his horse and in turn is killed by Mitchum. He gives tl
coup de grâce to his dying horse, then in long, lingering clos
ups he places his poncho, sombrero and gunbelt beside tl
dead Lacrimas and in a high angle long-shot walks down to tl
Rio Grande – to cross it and become an American. Tl
sequence achieves the ritual effect of a church service in whic
the priest seems to be painfully unfrocking himself to take on
new role. This is selfconsciously virtuoso film-making,

ourse (and one notes that director Robert Parrish served Ford, first as teenage actor in *The Informer* and later as an editor), but the virtuosity works to unite into a single compelling image the terrain, the highly charged décor and the movie's central theme.

Thirdly, there is the problem of anachronism. Without being a humourless pedant or a stickler for historical verisimilitude, one must raise the question as to how far a film-maker can disregard the known conditions of a period. Which is to say the most worked-over period of history as far as popular art is concerned and a relatively brief period of time concerning which – through the activities of local archives, pioneer museums, diaries, oral history programmes and so on – we have a quite extraordinary, almost embarrassing amount of knowledge. The easy answer perhaps is that in the field of historical romance we have to regard the Western as *sui generis*, that no laws can be laid down. On the one hand a film-maker can attempt to produce a pristine work reflecting the genuine currents of pioneer life derived straight from the archives of a state historical institute; on the other hand he may, like Sergio Leone and his European confrères, produce variations on the conventions of an established movie genre without having any personal roots in the actual culture which produced it. One way or another, anachronisms will occur – the genre is itself a charming anachronism. Yet somewhere between the past and the present lies the disruptive point where the Western no longer responds to our present needs or the too urgent demands made upon it, where the rituals and our understanding of them will destroy themselves. We do not appear to have reached that situation yet, but it would be foolhardy to believe that the genre is capable of such infinite renewal that such a time will not come.

2: Heroes and Villains, Women and Children

In that set of archetypes and expectations I have called the Model Western, the hero is the embodiment of good. He is upright, clean-living, sharp-shooting, a White Anglo-Saxon Protestant who respects the law, the flag, women and children; he dresses smartly in white clothes and rides a white horse which is his closest companion; he uses bullets and words with equal care, is a disinterested upholder of justice and uninterested in personal gain. He always wins. The villain, on the other hand, is the embodiment of evil; he dresses in black, rides a dark horse and is doomed to die. He is often a rather smooth talker and has lecherous designs on women; he is only concerned with advancing his own cause but beyond that has a positive commitment to destruction. The religious source of such a conflict is generally thought to be New England puritanism or American fundamentalism, its dramatic provenance taken as Victorian melodrama.

In the Western and popular culture generally we note the persistence of dramatic modes and types which have long since passed out of serious literature and high culture. H. J. Chaytor could almost have been talking about early cowboy movies when he wrote:

Mediaeval literature produced little formal criticism in our sense of the term. If an author wished to know whether his work was good or bad he tried it on an audience; if it was approved, he was soon followed by imitators. But authors were not constrained by models or systems, and independence or originality could enlarge and decorate any ground plan that had found general acceptance. Development proceeded by trial and error, the audience being the means of experiment. The audience wanted a story with plenty of action and movement; the story as a rule showed no great command of character drawing; this was left to the reciter for portrayal by change of voice and gesture. The story might contain or depend upon the most improbable coincidences or the wildest historical anachronisms; the audience would swallow them without demur. Unity of action could be provided by the use of allegory . . . or by emphasis upon love-motive . . . So, to appreciate the mediaeval narrative poem, we have to bear in mind that the women are peerless beauties, and the men are heroes dauntless among perils arising from foes often more than human . . .*

But as tastes have changed so has the character of the Western's *dramatis personae*. A certain complexity of motivation has marked occasional Westerns since silent days, but in the Forties and early Fifties the vogue for popular psychology and sociology swept Hollywood and came to challenge the simple moral basis of the Western. A striking early example of the Freudian Western was Raoul Walsh's *Pursued* (1947), where Robert Mitchum played a mentally disturbed cowboy torn by inner doubts caused by his status as an adopted child. Another was Henry Levin's *The Man From Colorado* (1948), in which Glenn Ford took the role of a psychotic judge. In a later, quite ludicrous movie, *The Fastest Gun Alive* (1956), the climax is a duel to determine who has the right to the film's title between a deranged outlaw (Broderick Crawford) whose wife has run off with a gunslinger, and a tormented storekeeper (Glenn Ford) who is haunted by childhood memories of failing to avenge the murder of his lawman father.

---

* *From Script to Print*: An Introduction to Medieval Vernacular Literature (Sidgwick and Jackson, London, 1966), p. 3.

Freudian Westerns: (*above*) Robert Mitchum as disturbed cowboy in *Pursued*; (*below*) Broderick Crawford as deranged outlaw in *The Fastest Gun Alive*

These are extreme but not atypical instances of the simple-minded attempts to make the genre more 'adult', to provide a substitute for a declining belief in good and evil; and they represent what is popularly and pejoratively understood as the 'psychological Western'. Heroes and villains alike became victims of their childhood and environment, neither good nor bad and often just 'sick'. The genre has never entirely recovered from this discovery nor completely given in to it. *Shane*, for example, has two parallel stories. On the one hand there is the social conflict between the hard-working farmers and the not unsympathetic rancher who is anxious to hang on to his open range; on the other hand there is the mythic confrontation between the tight-lipped, black-clad hired gun, Wilson (Jack Palance), who is the very incarnation of evil, and Shane, the buckskinned knight errant of the plains.

Perhaps one inevitable form of anachronism in the Western lies in attributing acceptable present-day motivations to these characters living in a historical context, however formalised. As Lionel Trilling has observed:

A characteristic of the literary culture of the post-Victorian age was the discovery that villains were not, as the phrase went, 'true to life', and that to believe in their existence was naïve. It became established doctrine that people were 'a mixture of good and bad' and that much of the bad could be accounted for by 'circumstances'. The diminished credibility of the villain, the opinion that he is appropriate only to the fantasy of melodrama, not to the truth of serious novels or plays, may in part be explained by the modern tendency to locate evil in social systems rather than in persons. But it is worth considering whether it might not have come about because the dissembling which defined the villain became less appropriate to new social circumstances than it had been to preceding ones. Perhaps it should not be taken for granted that the villain was nothing but a convention of the stage which for a time was also adopted by the novel. There is ground for believing that the villain was once truer to life than he later became.*

---

* *Sincerity and Authenticity* (Oxford University Press, London, 1972), p. 14.

Of course, the first person we think of in the Western is the hero – the cowboy, the Westerner. Not surprisingly the two best-known studies of the genre focus on him, as their titles suggest – Robert Warshow's *The Gentleman with a Gun* and Harry Schein's *Den Olympiske Cowboyen*. And in his essay 'Cowboys, Movies, Myths and Cadillacs', Larry McMurtry, author of the novel filmed as *Hud*, has proposed that we might employ Northrop Frye's terminology for fictional modes and categorise Westerns as 'high mimetic' or 'low mimetic' according to whether the hero is mythically apart from and superior to his fellow citizens or realistically on the same level as them.* I take McMurtry's point, but my own feeling is that to concentrate so much on the hero is misleading. First because a Western is defined by certain kinds of actions within a particular historical setting. Secondly because a picture is no less obviously a Western when the central character is an outlaw or an Indian, or when it has no definable hero at all, as is the case with Monte Hellman's *The Shooting* and Dick Richards' *The Culpepper Cattle Company*. Thirdly because the principal character is usually involved dramatically or psychologically with some opponent who may, depending upon the circumstances, possess greater charisma or social acceptance than himself.

Moreover the Western has come in recent years to challenge the very concept of heroism – not necessarily to destroy it, but to bring its traditional nature into question. Perhaps the most marked characteristic of the genre since the early Fifties has been its increasing emphasis not upon victory and success but upon losing – the suggestion that to remain true to oneself will almost invariably result in defeat: this in a society traditionally committed to success, to winning. Henry King's *The Gunfighter* and Brando's *One Eyed Jacks* are notable instances. In the latter, a gunman suggests to the Mexican hero Rio that

---

* *Man and the Movies*, ed. W. R. Robinson (Louisana University Press, Baton Rouge, 1967).

they should just go into town and kill their crooked opponent. 'That's not my style, Bob,' Rio replies. To which the gunman retorts, 'Then you better change your style, cos your style's a little slow.' Leaving aside the question that this might be a comment on the somewhat steady progress of the picture itself and the genre in general, we see here the notion of the hero becoming too good for this world. Instead of his triumph setting an example, his defeat and death become a rebuke to society. That is the message of most of Peckinpah's films. It is only in his superb study of a contemporary rodeo performer, *Junior Bonner* (1972), that he is able to treat the same theme unrestricted by the genre's demand for violent action; here he can let his victorious losers ride off into the sunset (the father onwards ever hopefully to a new frontier in Australia, the rueful, unembittered son driving his Cadillac and horse-trailer to yet another rodeo performance) instead of leaving them stretched out dead in the dust.

As winner or loser, as a mythic gunfighter like *Shane* or an accurately observed ageing cowhand like *Will Penny*, whether battling forces of existential evil or keeping the peace in the face of misunderstood delinquents, the Western hero nevertheless meets certain needs that other kinds of films and aspects of our culture fail to recognise or to satisfy in the same way. And when those needs are deliberately not fulfilled, when our expectations are deliberately frustrated, we are both upset and intrigued. Robert Lowell touched on this in reflecting on the courage of John Kennedy:

We have some sort of faith that the man who can draw most quickly is the real hero. He's proved himself. Yet that's a terribly artificial standard; the real hero might be someone who'd never got his pistol out of the holster and who'd be stumbling about and near-sighted and so forth. But we don't want to admit that. It's deep in us that the man who draws first somehow has proved himself. Kennedy represents a side of America that is appealing to the artist in retrospect, a certain heroism. And you feel, in certain terms, he really was a martyr in his death. He was reckless, went further than the office called for; perhaps you'd say that he was fated to be killed. And that's an image one could treasure and it stirs one.*

Lowell's comments on Kennedy – delivered off the cuff in conversation – invoke the immense complexity, the many-layered resonance of the Western hero's position. And as I have suggested, we cannot view him in isolation from his setting or his adversaries. It is not always easy to tell when Western moviemakers are unconsciously drawing on traditional mythology and when they are consciously constructing their plots from what Orson Welles (apologising for the 'Rosebud' motif in *Citizen Kane*) called 'dollar-book Freud'. Ultimately it does not really matter. The recurrent conflicts between fathers and sons (a son hunting a killer who turns out to be his own father in John Sturges' *Backlash*, or a father shooting down his own son in Phil Karlson's *Gunman's Walk*), between brothers competing to be the true heir to their father (Mann's *Winchester '73* and numerous other films), between former comrades-in-arms, between outlaws-turned-sheriff and their onetime companions, between the upright man and the evil brood ruled over by a self-righteous patriarch (*My Darling Clementine*, *Will Penny*, etc.) – all of these relationships can be traced back to traditional mythological sources. Equally they can be derived quite consciously from them. The extent to which the deep-dyed villain (Lee Marvin), the gunslinger (John Wayne) who shot him down, and the fumbling, greenhorn lawyer (James Stewart) who took the credit for his demise and went on to found a political career upon the deed, in John Ford's *The Man Who Shot Liberty Valance*, are symbolic, symbiotic figures is a matter of conjecture. As one of the crudest and at the same time most involved of Ford's Westerns, *Liberty Valance* is a genuine puzzle – the surface in fact is so

---

* A. Alvarez, *Under Pressure* (Penguin Books, London, 1965), p. 101.

Myth-making: Lee Marvin, James Stewart, John Wayne in *The Man Who Shot Liberty Valance*

unattractive that many observers (including Budd Boetticher, who has denounced it as a Ford misfire) have not been persuaded to penetrate this intriguing mess.

More easily accessible is *Cat Ballou*, featuring Marvin once again, but this time in the dual role of a deadly killer and a superannuated sheriff, who may be twin brothers. As becomes a confident satirist, Elliot Silverstein fully understood the relationship between the two, and equips them – in lightly handled vein – with the crucial flaws of their calling. The upright Kid Shelleen is a helpless drunk, his sense of vocation and social purpose lost until he is briefly redeemed, carefully prepared again for the knightly lists, wins, and returns once more to his drunken self-doubt. His evil *alter ego* Tim Strawn wears a tin cover to conceal his missing nose (the symbolic castration is pretty obvious) and can only express himself in violent action – he has no way of mediating his doubts. A

The Shooting: 'a strange mission into the desert'

companion of Cat Ballou refers to Tennyson ('Tennyson spins a good yarn, doesn't he?'), Cat herself carries a collected Tennyson concealing a Wild West dime novel, and Strawn's land-grabbing employer is an English nobleman (Reginald Denny) appropriately called Sir Harry Percival, suggesting none too subtly an element of Arthurian legend.

Less easy to pin down is Monte Hellman's *The Shooting*, where one cannot be sure within the exigencies of a chaotic, small budget production what was calculated and what fortuitous. Names like Leland Drum and Willet Gashade hazily invoke ancient nursery rhymes and more recent mythology. ('Aikin Drum' was the surrealist figure who 'lived in the moon' – traditionally a figure beyond death – in the Scottish ballad to which he gives his name; the last verse of the anonymous Western ballad *Jesse James* tells us that 'This song was made by Billy Gashade, As soon as the news did arrive.') In Hellman's film the bemused Gashade (Warren Oates) is hired by a woman to accompany her (and later an inscrutable gunman) on a strange mission into the desert culminating in a fatal, ambiguous confrontation between himself and a man who may or may not be his brother Coigne (Gashade's dying shout), but is certainly his *doppelgänger*. One wonders if it is carrying exegesis too far to suggest that 'Coigne' is a contraction of 'Cockaigne', the fabulous mythical place of idleness and plenty which America and the uncharted West was known as before, and for some time after, the voyage of Columbus.

During the credit titles of *How the West Was Won* the vast Cinerama screen is filled with the words 'The Civil War directed by John Ford'. The audience invariably laughs, I imagine. Yet at the same time they recognise a certain ironic truth. Of course Ford didn't do it entirely alone: indeed, the publicity handout for the picture insists that it would have been impossible 'for one director to carry the entire burden', and so an 'unprecedented' solution was arrived at in which 'three of Hollywood's most renowned directors, working in close co-ordination, shared the tremendous task', with the assistance of four top cinematographers and a cast of twenty-four stars. This may have been a lot for a single movie, but when one steps back from this epic production – and the shimmering lines that marked the joins between the Cinerama triptych encouraged the spectator to do so – one finds that a small, tight-knit group of familiar faces won the West, for the genre employs only a relative handful of directors, writers, cameramen and performers. One could draw up a roster of about fifty actors – fewer than the number of players under contract to the National Theatre and the Royal Shakespeare Company – who constitute the Western stock troupe, and between them their credits would include virtually every Western of any note (and a great many of no distinction) made over the past quarter of a century. A computer could reduce this to a much shorter list. Heroes: John Wayne, James Stewart, Henry Fonda, Gary Cooper, Randolph Scott, Joel McCrea, Glenn Ford as section one,

followed by Burt Lancaster, Richard Widmark, Rober
Mitchum, Gregory Peck, Charlton Heston, Kirk Douglas
Robert Taylor, Alan Ladd, Van Heflin, William Holden, Clin
Eastwood. Villains: Lee Marvin, Richard Boone, Robert Ryan
Arthur Kennedy, Dan Duryea, Edmond O'Brien, Nevill
Brand, John Dehner, Slim Pickens, Robert Wilke, Ian
Macdonald, Claude Akins, Lee Van Cleef, Jack Elam, Roya
Dano, Warren Oates, Anthony Quinn. Ranchers, sheriffs
deputies, sidekicks, assorted citizenry: Charles Bickford
Millard Mitchell, Edgar Buchanan, Ward Bond, Chill Wills
John Ireland, Walter Brennan, Ben Johnson, Harry Carey Jr
Noah Beery Jr, John McIntyre, Jay C. Flippen, Andy Devine
James Millican, Elisha Cooke Jr.

Taken along with the familiar plots and recurrent situations
these well-known, and increasingly well-worn, faces serve to
give the Western its quality of *déjà vu* and reinforce the sense o
ritual. The physical presence and established properties o
these actors have become part of the genre's iconography, to b
accepted literally or to be worked into new patterns or mined
for new meanings. Alone or in conflict with each other they
determine the tone of a picture, and most directors ar
intuitively aware of the way an actor's image and attributes ca
be manipulated and within what limits. Few of them are exactly
protean performers, though some are more versatile than
others.

John Wayne, for instance, could never figure in a movi
which demands much interior complexity in its hero; the com
plexity therefore, if sought, must come from the film's struc
ture, as in *The Searchers* or *The Man Who Shot Libert*
Valance. Randolph Scott is an even more rigid performer
whose course is unswerving if usually more concealed than
Wayne's. Inevitably he will make any group of crooks who join
up with him appear colourful, sometimes to the point of eccen
tricity (as in his Boetticher movies); still, there's something no
quite open about Scott's screen persona and in the right context

58

such as the Confederate agent he played in *Virginia City* (194
or the corrupt ex-lawman of *Guns in the Afternoon* (196
he can infuse colour into the essentially pallid performanc
of moral rectitude represented respectively in those filr
by Errol Flynn and Joel McCrea. Glenn Ford will impart a nc
of realism, intensity and ambiguity to the most simple mor
tale; where these elements are already present he can height
them to a rare degree, as in *3.10 to Yuma* (an apparent
realistic Western, though it is in fact a complex working c
of the Grail legend in the West) or *Day of the Evil Gun*,
take them over the edge until the film can seem neurot
cynical or absurd. Richard Boone's powerful villains threat
to overwhelm the forces of good; cast Boone on the side
society and you can almost dispense with a villain. Hen
Fonda, a true Westerner born in Nebraska, was rushed into t
genre in 1939 as the sympathetic outlaw Frank James in *Jes
James*, as a pioneer in the pre-Western *Drums Along t
Mohawk*, and as the future president in *Young Mr Lincol*
then repeated his outsider role in Fritz Lang's *Return of Frar
James* (1940) and William Wellman's realistic, anti-lynch la
The Ox-Bow Incident (1942), became confirmed as a key figu
in the Ford pantheon as upright Marshal Earp in *My Darlir
Clementine*, and in the late Sixties was ripe to be cast again as
sympathetic, ageing outlaw in *Firecreek* and a smiling, sadist
thug in the most ambitious of all Spaghetti Westerns, Serg
Leone's *Once Upon a Time in the West*. When Wayne is cast
a criminal there's usually a suggestion that something is wror
with the law in a local, easily resolved way; when Fonda is ca
as an outlaw the implication is that there's something basical
wrong with society. (Outside the Western, he fulfils this fur
tion in, for instance, *You Only Live Once*, *Grapes of Wrath* ar
The Wrong Man.)

The use of Fonda and Wayne proposes fairly immedia
social readings of the genre. Alan Ladd's performance in *Sha
is rather different. Perhaps no other actor could have given t

nething basically wrong with society ...': Fonda as outlaw in *Firecreek*

racter quite that quality of blank, ethereal detachment
ich Ladd brought to the part. He is like an angel in an
erwise realistic medieval painting, and sets off the earthy
lism of Van Heflin's father, Jean Arthur's unfulfilled pioneer
ther and Brandon de Wilde's deprived, yearning child. An
ntical film starring Wayne, Cooper or Stewart would have a
te different character. In hindsight, apart from being the
hetypal, highly stylised Western it seemed at the time (con-
ved of and accepted as 'classic'), *Shane* in many ways strikes
e as a forerunner of *Theorem* (1968), though far richer and
initely more congenial than Pasolini's disastrous little
egory. It is interesting to note that immediately before his
pearance as the deliberately unidentifiable spirit of something
other in *Theorem*, Terence Stamp starred as a doomed
tsider in a Western called *Blue* and as an English actor cast
a Spaghetti Western in 'Toby Dammit', Fellini's episode

of the Franco-Italian portmanteau picture *Histo*
Extraordinaires (1968).

This repertory of Western players has been getting ol
over the years, and many of them were not in their first flush
youth two decades ago. In consequence their very endurar
has given an increasing *gravitas* to the genre and has helped
compelled) the writing into it of the subject of ageing. A
product of this has been a curious shaping of the role
younger actors: excluding them, forcing them to adopt a mo
elderly mien, placing them in positions of tutelage, or sacri
ing them on the altar of inexperience. At its most extreme
are regaled with 121-year-old Dustin Hoffman in *Little*
Man, and Paul Newman's reappearance as a grizzled cent
arian to give the twentieth-century world its richly deserv
quietus at the end of John Huston's *The Life and Times*
Judge Roy Bean.

In the model, traditional Western there are two kinds
women. On the one hand there is the unsullied pioneer heroi
virtuous wife, rancher's virginal daughter, schoolteacher, e
on the other hand there is the saloon girl with her entourage
dancers. The former are in short supply, to be treated w
respect and protected. The latter are reasonably plentiful, s
ually available and community property. There is obviously
correspondence between these two groups and histori
actuality in the West – and an even greater connection betwe
them and the orthodox thinking of the late Victorian world
enshrined in Lord Baden-Powell's *Rovering to Success* (192
whose impressionable young readers were told that 'there a
women and there are dolls'. The two classes of women a
correspond, with the rewards and penalties their lives predict,
the demands of the Hollywood Production Code.

In archetypal form they appear as the cavalry officer's pre
nant wife (Louise Platt) and the banished saloon girl (Cla
Trevor) in Ford's *Stagecoach* (1939), whose passenger list

62

almost perfect cross-section of Western types – the two
omen, the chivalrous Southern gambler, the big-hearted
coholic doctor, the snooty, larcenous banker, the 'good' out-
w, the comic, prissy salesman, the jolly, uncomplicated
river, the gruff, sterling sheriff, with the cavalry and the
dians lurking ready to appear when needed. As custom dic-
tes, the officer's wife has the demure, WASPish name Lucy
allory, while the saloon girl bears the nickname 'Dallas'. (In
y Darling Clementine, for instance, the Eastern heroine is
med Clementine Carter and the saloon girl 'Chihuahua',
hile in *Destry Rides Again*, *Johnny Guitar* and *Rio Bravo*, the
orldly female leads played by Marlene Dietrich, Joan
rawford and Angie Dickinson are called, respectively if not
spectably, 'Frenchy', 'Vienna' and 'Feathers'.)

Just as all the other *Stagecoach* archetypes have been con-
antly reworked, so too have the women's roles changed. This
flects both a relaxation in censorship and the changing status
 women in society. Which is not to say that in the past every
estern was committed to these old conventions: the fact that
laire Trevor in *Stagecoach* is obviously a prostitute and gets
 marry the hero suggests that they were never exactly
andatory. This is however a fairly rare instance of relative
plicitness and an unusual case of a woman not having to pay
avily for her sins. Redemption in the Western, and in
ollywood films generally, has largely been a male prerogative.
illiam Wellman's otherwise unremarkable *Westward the
omen* (1952), which centres on a wagon-train of girls, mostly
 previous dubious virtue, being transported by an exasperated
ail boss, Robert Taylor, to marry sex-starved miners in
alifornia, is a singular, somewhat unedifying case of women
ing redeemed by the harsh experience of crossing a hostile
nd.

Now of course we have brothels clearly marked as such,
sorted to by hero and villain alike, and taking their place
ongside the saloon, the sheriff's office and the livery stable as

one of the essential amenities of any Western town. By 1970
was even possible to set a whole film in one, as was the cas
with Gene Kelly's *The Cheyenne Social Club*, the ultimat
whores' opera, where James Stewart inherits a bawdy house i
Wyoming to his, and also the audience's, embarrassment. Th
liberation here, if it be such, is not that of women but of film
makers from old moral standards.

Just as one cannot any longer tell the good guys from th
bad guys, one cannot with quite the same ease distinguis
between the good girls and the bad girls. A striking instance
to be found in Ted Post's *Hang 'Em High* (1968), a stol
Western with a fashionable line in bondage and necrophili
reminiscent of the same director's *Legend of Tom Doole*
(1957). The hero (Clint Eastwood), who spends a good deal
time consorting with whores, is rather surprised when the film
store-keeping heroine (Inger Stevens) constantly rebuffs h
advances. It transpires that she isn't an old-fashioned gi
protecting her virtue but is suffering from frigidity as th
consequence of a traumatic group rape. From this affliction th
hero cures her one suitably stormy night.

These changes – made possible, in some cases insisted upo
by Hollywood's increasing permissiveness – have occasionall
led to the depiction of more mature relations between the sexe
and the appearance of many an anachronistically liberate
woman on the range; but the Western remains a man's worl
Yet it is no longer possible merely to accept the solitariness an
implied misogyny of the Westerner: questions of sex and th
single cowboy must be explained or demonstrated. In th
Randolph Scott–Budd Boetticher movies, for example, Sco
was almost invariably presented as a widower, and in thre
cases (*Seven Men From Now*, *Decision at Sundown* and *Ri*
Lonesome) he was actually seeking revenge on the men wh
killed his wife. In Sam Peckinpah's movies the heroes rare
meet any women except whores, and one cannot escape th
implication that in the director's view prostitutes have a great

64

honesty than other women. Beneath the surface of fashion a
the veneer of realism in so many recent films, we could
seeing confirmation of what has long been thought about o
shared aspect of most Western heroes. Which is to say th
while not necessarily a latent homosexual, the hero secre
fears women and the civilisation, compromise and settled l
they represent; he sees them as sources of corruption a
betrayal, luring him away from independence and a sure sense
himself as well as from the more comforting company of me

If the Western is the supremely male Hollywood genre, t
Musical is its feminine counterpart or complement. Wh
rather pallid males like Gene Autry and Roy Rog
dominated that now thankfully defunct form, the 'Singi
Western', the 'Western Musical', altogether a more *ad hoc*, le
run-of-the-production-line thing, was largely the province
female stars. On stage (Ethel Merman) and screen (Be
Hutton) it was the sharp-shooting Miss Oakley who drew fi
in *Annie Get Your Gun* (1950), even if she was subsequen
forced to conceal her talents to get her man; and in what
virtually a pastiche of Irving Berlin's Broadway triump
David Butler's likeable *Calamity Jane* (1953), Doris Day r
only took centre stage but rode shotgun as well.

She was soon followed by Rosemary Clooney in Geor
Marshall's mildly satirical *Red Garters* (1954), and a few yea
later by Debbie Reynolds in Vincent Sherman's *The Seco
Time Around* (1961). She was long preceded, however, by Ju
Garland in what is possibly the best Western Musical, Geor
Sidney's *The Harvey Girls* (1946), a tribute to those intrep
New England ladies who went West in the late nineteer
century to provide miners and cowboys with an infinit
superior service and cuisine than that to which they had be
accustomed. The Fred Harvey Company, as a sub-division
the Amtrac Organisation, is still a part of the living We
having a monopoly of hospitality around the Grand Cany
and on the edges of the Navajo Reservation. *The Harvey G*

Women in the West: Mercedes McCambridge in *Johnny Guitar*

contains the finest musical tribute to the technological pioneers of the West in the bravura presentation of Johnny Mercer's number 'The Atchison, Topeka and the Santa Fe'.

Westerns of course have to feature women if only because commercial movies must offer some so-called romantic inter-est. When women take the centre of the stage in this most masculine of genres, the result is less likely to be a blow in favour of sexual equality than a strong whiff of erotic perver-ity. I don't refer here to actresses who have given major and memorable performances in traditional roles: Marlene Dietrich's saloon girls in *Destry Rides Again* (1939) and *Rancho Notorious* (1952), Jean Arthur's farm-wife in *Shane*, Angie Dickinson's singer in *Rio Bravo* (1959), Diane Cilento's tough hotel proprietress in *Hombre* (1967), Maureen O'Hara in half a dozen movies, to name but a few examples of the opportunities which, contrary to accepted opinion, the Western has afforded to actresses over the years. What I mean are those

movies which cast women in essentially masculine roles a
outlaw leaders or as ranch bosses: Miss Barbara Stanwyck
leading exponent of the all-American bitch, in several films
most notably Samuel Fuller's *Forty Guns* (1957); her close
rival Joan Crawford doing battle with Mercedes McCambridg
in Arizona in Nicholas Ray's much admired *Johnny Guita*
(1953); Jeanne Crain as a ruthless cattle queen in King
Vidor's *Man Without a Star* (1955). The effect of such casting
is invariably to produce a quality of savagery, heartlessness
heavy-handed eroticism and extravagant sexual symbolism and
innuendo, bordering on the risible. Some might think this
outcome only too predictable, since it is indeed a literal
travesty of the Western. In addition, it diverts women from
their principal dramatic role in cowboy movies – as well as in
most male action movies for that matter – which is to be the
voice of reason speaking out against violence, its character
building function, and the idea that human affairs can be settled
by force.

Perhaps this view is an unrealistic and sentimental one, and
it could be argued that my criticisms of these films – par
ticularly *Man Without a Star* – are in fact the very points they
are actually making. That this is the case with the eponymous
heroine played by Jane Fonda in *Cat Ballou* (1965) is certain
but that film is perhaps the only comedy Western worth taking
seriously as a genuine, well-observed satire on the genre. The
ugly, role-reversing phenomenon of the belligerent, gun-happy
woman is given a good deal of conscious critical attention in
Burt Kennedy's stark allegorical fable *Welcome to Hard Time*
(1966), where a likeable, hard-hearted Irish whore (Janice
Rule) despises her lover, the town's pacifist mayor (Henry
Fonda), and ensures that her adopted son is instructed in the
use of guns so that he will be able to kill the madman who had
raped her. The result is that when the rapist eventually returns
not only is the boy's instructor shot dead, but she herself is
accidentally killed when the boy takes his rifle to protect her

So much, the film implies, for women who step outside their appointed role; and so much too, one senses, for the American housewives (so vividly depicted at small-arms classes in Haskell Wexler's *Medium Cool*) who assiduously take shooting lessons and turn their suburban homes into arsenals.

Whatever may be happening in other branches of the cinema, the Western remains a place dominated by men, and mostly men of fairly mature years. The juvenile delinquent doesn't last long. If he pulls a gun, for instance, as the wild youngster played by Russ Tamblyn does in *Cimarron* (1960), he'll soon be stretched out in the morgue instead of going to reform school or, like Skip Homeier (the archetypal Hitler Youth in the wartime propaganda movie *Tomorrow the World*, who graduated to being the West's archetypal Peter Pan thug) who shot Johnny Ringo in the back in *The Gunfighter*, he'll briefly inherit a doomed reputation. If he joins a gang of fellow tearaways, he may well find himself up against not only an unbeatable sheriff but an ageing outlaw as well, as in *The Good Guys and the Bad Guys*.

In a rather old-fashioned way, the Western assumes that young people have a lot to learn from their elders and very little to teach them, and that the process of learning is long and painful, that a man must prove himself in a variety of rituals before he can take his place in adult society. The Western is in fact a highly didactic form, and so prominent is this pedagogic strain that it seems to disprove Keats' assertion that we hate that which 'has a palpable design upon us'. As the fleeing judge in *High Noon* hastily packs his belongings, he tells Marshal Kane that this is 'no time for a lesson in civics, boy'. In this he is mistaken. Whatever else may have to be set aside in the Western, there is always time for a little instruction. Not surprisingly, one of the few harbingers of civilisation that the Westerner traditionally respects is the schoolteacher: in *The Gunfighter*, Ringo's estranged wife is a schoolmarm; in *Man of the West*, the interrupted journey which brings Gary Cooper back to his old gang has as its object the hiring of a teacher; in *The Big Country* the voice of reason, courted by both sides in a range war, is schoolmarm Jean Simmons; and so on. Unquestionably the nastiest character in Charles Haas' brilliant, highly stylised little Western *Star in the Dust* (1956) is the local schoolteacher, a man of some intelligence and organising ability who throws himself into a range war on the side of the farmers against the ranchers to further his political ambitions. 'I'm not cut out to be an underpaid schoolteacher all my life,' he says, setting aside the disinterested attitude expected of him. (Close students of subtle Hollywood casting methods will note that he is played by the same slightly sinister actor, Robert Osterloh, who was shot dead in his classroom by a home-made zip-gun wielded by one of his pupils in *City Across the River* made in 1949, one of Hollywood's earliest and most sensational juvenile delinquency pictures.)

Normally, when his actions are questioned, the Western hero will answer with a laconic 'There are some things a man can't ride around' or 'A man's got to do what a man's got to do' or 'Well, if you don't know, I can't tell you.' Faced with a child or an adolescent, however, he feels obliged to pass on what he knows about life, which frequently comes down to matters of handling guns, women, cattle and drink – especially guns. For every Showdown at Wichita there's a little Teach-In in Dodge City.

In *Shane*, the eponymous hero (Alan Ladd) explains to the little boy Joey how to use a pistol. 'Some like to have two guns but one's all you need if you know how to use it ... A gun is as good or bad as the man using it,' he says, and in a burst of furious shooting he reveals how close the honourable gunman is to the killer. In *Man Without a Star*, the hero takes a young Easterner under his wing to show him the ropes, and the film's subplot turns on the way this young man initially goes astray by only aping his master's external style before attaining self-mastery. Similarly, in Peckinpah's *Guns in the Afternoon*, a

'The pedagogic strain': Alan Ladd and Brandon De Wilde in *Shane*

cocky young gunman who has learned his skills from or master, discovers how to use them responsibly from anothe (He is also upbraided for littering the countryside, and und the stern eye of his mentor retrieves a piece of paper ar pockets it.) One of the most remarkable instances of the han ing on of gun lore is to be found in Phil Karlson's *Gunman Walk* (1958). Here a prosperous, middle-aged rancher (Va Heflin – combining his own stolid farmer role from *Shane* wi Alan Ladd's panache) has two sons, one of whom is du decent and pacific, the other strident, attractive and tough. Th first has his father's stability and integrity but none of the sk and ruthlessness which enabled him to establish himself in tl pioneer West. The second son has the father's drive and styl but none of the inner balance. The father tends to view one wi guarded contempt and love the other, but an early scene shooting practice explosively demonstrates that the weak be who loathes shooting is best equipped for life now that tl frontier has closed, and that the apparently strong boy, wl revels in guns, has inherited a dangerously outmoded style ai outlook. This early realisation is amply confirmed by the boy anti-social conduct, and finally in a climactic gunfight the fath is forced to kill his own son – which in symbolic terms involv killing part of himself.

One of the more likeable aspects of the sadistic *Neva Smith* (1966) is the emphasis on the hero's education. F learns to shoot from a travelling gunsmith who tells him th 'handling the things is only part of it – the other part is learni to know human nature.' Subsequently the wild young Smi (Steve McQueen) discovers how to drink, play poker, hand whores and bide his time. He even takes up reading and there a nice touch when his life is preserved by a copy of a readi primer he carries in his pocket. 'The McGuffey Reader sav your heart,' the doctor tells him. Regrettably the object of this instruction is only to track down and despatch in singularly brutal way the murderers of his parents.

ys into men: John Wayne and pupils in *The Cowboys*

Such instruction has a clearly symbolic purpose – to teach
dgment, self-restraint, self-sufficiency, a code of conduct and
orality which goes with the acquiring of character. In the case
f a picture like *Nevada Smith*, though, the purpose to which
e education is put is only too literally an extension of the very
ature of the instruction itself – killing, revenge, the assertion
f character in terms of primitive machismo. The hero's inevit-
le satiation and disgust with killing is hardly a substitute for
nuine irony. Nor is much irony to be found in Mark Rydell's
he Cowboys (1972), where John Wayne is forced to recruit a
am of innocent adolescents to conduct his cattle drive and
troduces them to guns, whores, drinking and killing.
omehow they have become men, and when Wayne is gunned
wn they can carry on his task and dispose of his murderers in
ultant fashion.

A much sharper, more critical account of the situation in
he Cowboys is to be found in Dick Richards' excellent *The*

Culpepper Cattle Company, which appeared at much the sam
time. Here we see a 16-year-old Texan (Gary Grimes) joinin
an arduous cattle drive out of a romantic desire to live tl
cowboy's life. He too becomes a man, but the film's authors
and to a lesser extent the boy himself – show real awareness
the kind of man he is becoming as he is initiated into tl
squalid pleasures, the self-seeking, the random violence arouı
him. Without ever making it too explicit, Richards seems to
implying that the Culpepper Cattle Company is America –
business ploughing relentlessly on, totally amoral, fightiı
when it must, compromising when it can, a few deranged
misguided members galloping off from time to time to purs
'idealistic' Vietnam-like missions on the side which neith
adversary nor apparent beneficiary justifies.

Apart from their presence *in statu pupillari*, and to affo
their elders the opportunity of passing on the bruised fruits
their experience, children fulfil other roles in the Western. On
naturally, is a decorative function in contributing to the sen
of community. Another more dramatic role is to act as
ironic comment upon the action. In *High Noon*, as Marsh
Kane goes about his vain attempt to enlist the aid of his fellc
citizens, the kids in the street anticipate the climax by playing
little game called 'Bang Bang, you're dead, Kane'. In *T
Gunfighter*, the children are full of dime novel talk abo
Western heroes, and stare through the window at the legenda
Johnny Ringo as he sits in the saloon under a steel engraving
Custer's Last Stand. When Ringo sees his own son, from whc
he has been long absent, he discovers that the boy's hero
Wyatt Earp. In a pre-credit sequence to Allen Miner's *T
Ride Back* (1957), a child playing in an empty street with a t
gun seems to have fired a real shot, until the sudden revelati
that the noise came from the pistol of bandit Anthony Qui
running for his life.

There is thus a triple role for children: being trained
take their place in society; being caught up in, and possi

74

rrupted by, the Western myth and the mystique of frontier
olence; reminding us that the aggressive instinct and a fascin-
on with violence are things we are born with. In no movie-
ker's work is this given more prominence than in that of
m Peckinpah, who was himself brought up in the West as the
scendant of pioneer grandparents. In his first movie, *The
eadly Companions*, the hero accidentally shoots a little boy
o has come out to get a better view of a bank robbery; the
urney which forms the dramatic spine of the picture is made
his mother to bury him in a remote town beside his father.
the opening sequence of *Guns in the Afternoon*, emphasis is
en to the mollycoddling attention of mothers to their over-
essed children in a turn-of-the-century Californian town on
ich civilisation has imposed its baleful hand in the form of
eet-lamps, horseless carriages, uniformed cops; and by impli-
ion their conformism is contrasted with the opportunities a
ung gunman and a farmgirl have of learning about life from
o old marshals with whom they ride into the mountains away
m the town. In *Major Dundee*, the first thing children do
er being released from their Apache captors is to play with
ws and arrows, and it is real guns they look at with wide-
ed fascination in *The Wild Bunch*; at the end one of them
oots William Holden in the back.

3: Indians and Blacks

I have spoken earlier of 1950 being the watershed year
which the Western took on a new depth, seriousness a
resonance. This change was most marked in the treatment
the Indian, whose predicament was at the centre of the fi
Westerns directed by Anthony Mann and Delmer Daves. I
the word 'Indian' here and elsewhere with the embarrass
knowledge that the term is considered offensive by present-c
descendants of the original Americans, though they have yet
agree among themselves upon an acceptable description. Hc
ever, Leslie Fiedler has suggested in *The Return of
Vanishing American* that all American literature can be divic
into Northerns, Southerns, Easterns and Westerns, and t
stories set in the West which do not involve Indians
'unfulfilled occasions for myth rather than myth itself':

The heart of the Western is not the confrontation with the a
landscape (by itself this produces only the Northern), but the enco
ter with the Indian, that utter stranger for whom our New Worl
an Old Home, that descendant of neither Shem nor Japheth, nor e
like the Negro imported to subdue the wild land, Ham.*

In Fiedler's analysis the hero of the New England-set North
is transformed into a Yankee; the hero of the Southern, throu

* Jonathan Cape, London, 1969, p. 16.

s confrontation with the Negro or the spirit of blackness,
turned into 'Whitey'; in the Eastern he becomes a déraciné
smopolitan or a tourist who heads home. In the Western,
wever,

e tensions of the encounter are resolved by eliminating one of the
ythological partners – by ritual or symbolic means in the first
stance, by physical force in the second. When the first method is
ed, possibilities are opened up for another kind of Western, a
condary Western dealing with that New Man, the American *ter-*
m quid; but when the second is employed – our home grown Final
lution – the Western disappears as a living form, for the West has,
effect, been made into an East.

To return to the less heady world of Hollywood in 1950,
nthony Mann's film was *Devil's Doorway*, in which a
oshone brave, symbolically named Broken Lance (Robert
aylor) returns from distinguished service in the Civil War to
d himself an alien in his own Wyoming home. 'Under the law
u're not classed as an American citizen – you're a ward of
e American government,' he is told, and at the climax of the
m he dons his old army uniform to die a defeated man,
ough saying to a sympathetic lady lawyer with whom a
ntative romance has been suggested, 'Don't worry, Anne – a
ndred years from now it might have worked.'
Throughout the film Taylor is presented as an unblemished
ro and is always photographed in such a manner (for
ample, low angle shots against the sky or lit from behind) as
make him dominate the scene. The same is true of Jeff
handler's appearance as Cochise, the peace-loving Apache
ader in Daves' *Broken Arrow*, which also made a serious, if
lf-conscious, attempt to present Indian life with sympathy
d some authenticity. In this case, however, the film ends with
e suggestion of permanent peace, but only after the death of
ochise's daughter. No doubt she had to die as punishment
r the crime of miscegenation, for she had married a cavalry

'A serious, if self-conscious, attempt to present Indian life with sympathy . . .': Del
Paget, James Stewart, Jeff Chandler in *Broken Arrow*

scout (James Stewart), the movie's instrument of raci
reconciliation.

The considerable impact of these pictures (*Broken Arro*
proved one of the year's most successful and widely discuss
films) has to be seen against the then established role of t
Indian in the Western. Conventionally the redskin has been o
of the hazards facing those bent on taming a continent a
winning the West. At best he was the noble savage of Fenimo
Cooper, sharing the same qualities of primitive grandeur whi
resided in the challenge of the wild terrain and harsh climat
At worst he followed a tradition established by early Victori
melodrama: he was treacherous, bloodthirsty, uncompromi
ing, threatening rape, mutilation and death.

The depiction of Indians before 1950 was not alwa
unsympathetic. Back in 1912, D. W. Griffith's *The Massac*
showed them as hapless victims of an unprovoked cavalry rai

James Cruze's *Covered Wagon* (1923) made clear that they were motivated by a reasonable desire to protect their hunting grounds; *The Vanishing American* (1925) sketched a history of the American Indian from early cliff-dwelling days up to the ignominious death of a World War I Indian hero (Richard Dix) back on his neglected reservation. Indeed the historians of the genre, George N. Fenin and William K. Everson, in their book *The Western*, argue that in the early days of the silent era 'the Indian was seen as a hero almost as frequently as the white man, but already there was a difference. He seemed more of a symbol, less an individual than the cowboy.'

This faceless symbol became a stereotype: historically a figure to be confronted and defeated in the name of civilisation, dramatically a terrifying all-purpose enemy ready at the drop of a tomahawk to spring from the rocks and attack wagon trains, cavalry patrols and isolated pioneer settlements. Unlike other racial minorities or foreigners, the Indian was unprotected by the Hays Office Code, box-office caution, or political influence. There has of course never been a shortage of crooked traders or Indian-hating officers to provoke conflict and also serve as scapegoats for the white race. But this, I think, is also part of the film-makers' approach to their subject, for the Indian could not even serve as an individually realised villain.

The liberal, anti-racist cycle which followed *Devil's Doorway* and *Broken Arrow* has continued unabated up to the present. But if Hollywood made token amends to the Apache, the Sioux, the Cheyenne and a dozen other tribes well before Edmund Wilson made his celebrated *Apologies to the Iroquois* in 1960, the Indian stereotype has not so much been shattered as reshaped. The immediate successors to *Broken Arrow* were mostly content to repeat that apparent breakthrough, trading in an easy optimism that blithely rewrites history in terms of reconciliation and peaceful coexistence, like *Sitting Bull* (1954), *The White Feather* (1955) and *The Indian Fighter*

79

Apache: Burt Lancaster as fugitive Indian

(1955), or giving a perfunctory nostalgic shrug as in *Hondo* (1954). A few pictures attempted to go rather deeper. Particularly memorable are the opening sequences of Robert Aldrich's *Apache* (1954), where a garish white civilisation is seen through the eyes of a fugitive Indian (Burt Lancaster) making his way back West after escaping from a deportation train taking him to exile in Florida. A tragic ending was planned for this picture, but the front office insisted on optimism and this is what the makers delivered in a hopelessly unconvincing way.

So, for all the fine liberal sentiment, the Indian remained one of the pawns in the Western game, to be cast in whatever role the film-maker chose. Commercially this was inevitable, and an aesthetic case can be made out (indeed, frequently has been) against too drastic a change in the genre's established conventions. Clearly, from around 1950 the Indian in the contemporary allegorȳ can stand for the Negro when the implications are social or for the Communist when the implications are political, though generally the identification is somewhat woolly. *Broken Arrow* obviously could be viewed as a plea for racial tolerance on a domestic level and for peaceful coexistence on an international one. The same is true of numerous other movies which followed it: during the McCarthy era Hollywood artists were often forced to turn to allegory to handle themes which the studio bosses would have rejected as too controversial in a modern setting.

Of course the natural tendency of the Western is 'hawkish', whatever the pacific intention of its individual exponents. Consequently a movie like Charles Marquis Warren's *Arrowhead* (1953), however distasteful it may seem beside its liberal contemporaries, had a charge which was largely lacking in many well-meaning pictures of its time, as well as not appearing to impose worthy latterday sentiments on to earlier situations. The central character, an Indian-hating cavalry scout called Ed Bannon (Charlton Heston), was apparently based on a real-life scout, Al Sieber, and it is with astonishment that we realise that he is the film's authentic hero, leading a drive to put down the ghost-dancing heresy as it sweeps through Texas. For neither the first nor the last time in a Western the ghost-dance movement, contrary to all historical evidence, is presented as a violent insurrectionist activity instead of the largely pacifist one that it was. The leader of the uprising is the Apache chief Torriano (Jack Palance), who returns from an Eastern college to arouse his people. There is a striking image as Torriano arrives home in immaculate white man's clothing and removes his stetson to shake down a mane of black hair, a good dozen years before such a hair-style became the badge of the disaffected young. Virtually his next act is to kill his blood brother, a Wells Fargo agent.

Arrowhead ends with a terrifying hand-to-hand fight in which Bannon breaks Torriano's neck and with it his influence. 'There's your inviolable one,' he says to the Indian's distraught followers. While I have no idea what the conscious motivation of the writer-director were, the picture strikes me as an ultr right-wing allegory of the McCarthy period in which th Indians – and especially the college-educated Torriano brin ing his heresy from the East – do service for Communists, an the whites, with their unwavering leader Bannon, for those re blooded American patriots bent on rooting out the Communi conspiracy at home and standing up to its menace abroad.

There are relatively few Westerns of the past twenty year which take such an overtly hostile attitude towards the Indian as *Arrowhead*. It is generally the role of a white villain to ech the 1869 sentiment of General Sheridan that 'the only goo Indian is a dead Indian.' On the other hand there must be man people who would agree with the opinion expressed in a 197 *Playboy* interview by John Wayne, who has spent much of hi life fighting Indians on the screen:

I don't feel we did wrong in taking this great country away fror them. There were great numbers of people who needed new land, an the Indians were selfishly trying to keep it for themselves.

The movies are after all an expression of the dominant cultur Consequently the Indians are invariably viewed, whether syn pathetically or not, from the point of view of the victoriou pioneers and their White Anglo-Saxon Protestant societ When serious doubts arise about this culture, however, th Indian will be viewed in a different light. I shall be touchin later on the gradual movement in this direction.

But in passing one should perhaps say something about th neglect in the American cinema of the plight of the contempor ary Indian. There have been touching if evasive accounts of th sad lives of the 1912 Olympic champion Jim Thorpe, the Sac Fox Indian from Oklahoma who was stripped of his athleti honours after being charged with infringing his amateur statu by accepting money for summer baseball games in colle

(*Jim Thorpe – All American* in 1951 with Burt Lancaster as Thorpe), and of the World War II hero Ira Hayes, the Pima Indian from Arizona who took to drink back on his neglected Arizona reservation (*The Outsider*, 1952, starring Tony Curtis). In the years of his pathetic decline Thorpe appeared in several low-grade Westerns of the Thirties, and in 1950 Ira Hayes was called to Hollywood to re-create the famous flag-raising tableau in the John Wayne movie *The Sands of Iwo Jima*.*

A number of TV documentaries have exposed the Indians' situation, and in 1962 there was Kent McKenzie's *The Exiles*, an unsatisfactory study of the pathetic, déraciné Indian poor in Los Angeles, which had its moments but suffered from the director's inability to get his non-professional cast to act out their lives in a convincing fashion. More recently there has been Carol Reed's *The Last Warrior* (1970), a well-intentioned film about Indian resistance on a present-day reservation which went disastrously astray through the unbridled performance of Anthony Quinn doing another of his boozy, outsize, life-force figures, in this case a sort of Arizona Zorba the Navajo. And the equally well intentioned, and only slightly more successful *Billy Jack* (1971), written and directed (under the pseudonym T. C. Frank) by Tom Laughlin, who also plays the eponymous hero, a half-Indian Vietnam war veteran wandering around Arizona and becoming idealistically involved in a hopelessly melodramatic fashion with reservation Indian radicals and white counter-culturists. The subject is promising, but despite some pungent satire provided by the San Francisco Committee company, the execution is unsatisfactory.

---

* A much better version of the Ira Hayes story is, I'm told, John Frankenheimer's TV film *The American* (with Lee Marvin as Hayes), in which the doomed hero's life is unfolded in flashback as he staggers drunkenly around the set during the filming of *The Sands of Iwo Jima*. A description of this film is to be found in *Only You Dick Daring* by Merle Miller, who wrote the teleplay.

On an altogether higher plane from *The Last Warrior* and *Billy Jack* stands *When the Legends Die* (1972), the first movie to be directed by Stuart Millar,. producer of Arthur Penn's *Little Big Man*. Millar's film, which belongs to the current cycle of rodeo movies, in some ways resembles Robert Rossen's *The Hustler* in its story of an ageing alcoholic cowboy (Richard Widmark) who trains a 19-year-old Southern Ute Indian, Thomas Black Bull (Frederick Forrest), in broncobusting and takes him round small-town rodeos to cheat the local gamblers. But what the picture is really about is the rejection of contemporary America and the success ethic by Tom Black, who has gained a reputation as a 'killer' for the ferocious way he rides and punishes the animals he was raised to love and care for. Through his eyes we experience the disfigured Western landscape, the phoney patriotic charades of the rodeo circuit, and the lurking prejudice and meanness surrounding him. In one of the film's highpoints we see him crouching with his hat on at a garish indoor rodeo as the band strikes up the National Anthem. Slowly, reluctantly, he rises among his fellow competitors, eventually removes his stetson and brings it to his heart with a contemptuous slap. At the beginning of the film he had been unwillingly brought to a coldly sterile boarding school for Indian reservation orphans, and his elderly guardian-translator informed, 'Tell him that we will listen to what he has to say about the old ways when he has learnt the new ways.' At the end he quits the rodeo business and returns 'to be with the horses'. 'I've learned the new ways,' he says wearily – a 23-year-old veteran who wants nothing more than to drop not out but back into his counter-culture.

This should be a growth area in the Western genre, and the material for a potential masterpiece is lurking there waiting for the right artist to shape it. However, the fact that Indian tribes in New Mexico are now financing movies does not necessarily mean that the pictures they back will be revolutionary in character. On the contrary, current projects suggest that they are putting their money into conventionally conservative Western fare.

Still, my real concern here is with the treatment of the Indians in Western movies, which is a complex enough subject in itself, if admittedly trivial when set alongside what is happening in the slums and reservations of contemporary America.

Two dominant traits during the Fifties and early Sixties were on the one hand the role of the Indians as an external force in uniting Americans and on the other the cultural clash between pioneer and redskin. In pictures as crude as John Sturges' *Escape from Fort Bravo* (1953) and as subtle as Sam Peckinpah's *Major Dundee* (1965), we have seen murderously divided parties of Northern soldiers and their Confederate prisoners drawn together in a new sense of national solidarity in the face of Indian attack. This has become almost a cliché. The other category is more interesting: those movies which deal with whites living among Indians and Indians (usually, but not always, half-castes) attempting to get along in white society. The major examples of this species are John Huston's *The Unforgiven* (1960) and Don Siegel's *Flaming Star* (1960), where white families stand together to protect an adopted Indian sister (Audrey Hepburn in *The Unforgiven*) or half-breed brother (Elvis Presley in *Flaming Star*) from rejection by white society or reclamation by the redskins. Thematically they are declarations in favour of the American melting pot; dramatically they are a recognition of the profound difficulties and personal tragedies involved in the process of assimilation. A far more complex approach to similar issues is to be found in Robert Mulligan's *The Stalking Moon* (1968), an extraordinarily ferocious metaphysical Western with a strong Lawrentian undertow, in which a retired cavalry scout (Gregory Peck) and an unseen Indian chief struggle for the allegiance and cultural identity of the Indian's mute, half-breed son. I mention Lawrence here because few films so directly bring up the issues he raised in *Studies in Classic American Literature*, and few pictures have so consciously exploited the naked power of the symbolic Indian.

A rather different emphasis from *The Unforgiven* and *Flaming Star* is revealed in films about white settlers embarking on expeditions to regain members of their families captured by Indians, which are testimony to the fragility of white civilisation. These pictures raise the questions – Can these prisoners, even if located, be rehabilitated? and, Will the seekers themselves remain the same? In the last couple of years more robust and optimistic answers have been given to these questions – or rather the nature of the questions themselves has been challenged. But in the Fifties there was an underlying anxiety about them, and they are to be found at the centre of John Ford's *The Searchers* (1956), a film of great charm and much crudity dominated by the cultural assurance of John Wayne, and the same director's *Two Rode Together* (1961), where Ford took a more pessimistic view of the effects of captivity but at the same time showed greater sympathy for the captors and the culture into which the white women and children had fallen. I don't think one is reading too much into these films in seeing them as expressing a fear about the possible breakdown of American society in the face of an underlying drive towards anarchy and disintegration, a feeling that the inhabitants of America have a tenuous grasp upon their continent.

One dominant direction of the Western during the postwar period, and increasingly in the Sixties, lay in setting movies at the very end of the frontier period, and thus confronting the old virtues of the West with the corrupt values of the burgeoning twentieth-century commercial civilisation. This was taken to its extreme in William Fraker's *Monte Walsh* (1970), in which the ageing cowhands are presented quite explicitly as victims of anonymous corporations ultimately controlled from Wall Street. In most of these films Indians in their post-Wounded Knee subjugation are notable by their absence. The only major

Western dealing centrally with the Indian during this post-frontier period is Abraham Polonsky's *Tell Them Willie Boy is Here* (1969), which tells the true story of a Paiute outcast who in 1909 was hounded to death in a chase across Southern California by a posse of vindictive whites after the accidental killing of his girlfriend's father. It is played out against a background of unyielding racial intolerance and social indifference, as well as the concurrent visit to the West by President Taft, which led to insane rumours of assassination threats and a massive Indian uprising.

The Indian as perennial outsider – as represented by *Willie Boy* – is not a new theme in the Western. One can go back to a picture which appeared in the same year as *Broken Arrow* to find the Indian presented in terms of parity with Mormons, fugitive gunfighters and travelling entertainers, as social outcasts within the implied framework of an intolerant American conformity. This movie is John Ford's *Wagonmaster*. In a sense, Indians have always been outsiders in Ford's films, though his treatment of them, except in *Wagonmaster* and his last Western, *Cheyenne Autumn*, has always been an embarrassing subject for his admirers, despite the increasing sympathy which parallels his decreasingly sanguine attitude to the contemporary world. Peculiarly offensive now, if little remarked on at the time, and fairly reflecting his earlier attitude, is the sequence in *My Darling Clementine* (1946) where Wyatt Earp (Henry Fonda) asserts his claim to the moral and civic leadership of Tombstone by going into a saloon, from which the frightened patrons have fled, to arrest a drunken, gun-toting Indian. 'What kind of town is this – selling whisky to Indians?' he demands scornfully. Moreover he doesn't even bother to put his pathetic prisoner in jail, but casually kicks him in the rump, saying, 'Indian – get out of town and stay out.' The Indian in effect has no place in the community which Earp is shaping.

This is the way that villains are established today, not heroes. Fourteen years after *My Darling Clementine* and a decade after *Wagonmaster*, John Sturges' *The Magnificent Seven* establishes the liberal credentials and nonconformity of the Seven's leaders (Yul Brynner and Steve McQueen) through an opening scene in which they take over a hearse carrying the body of a dead Indian, drive it up to the white cemetery and force a hostile racist community to accept the Indian for burial there. More recently we have seen Martin Ritt's *Hombre* (1967), whose eponymous white hero (Paul Newman) has been reared as a child by Indians, grown to manhood in white society and subsequently elected to live as an Indian. Nothing is vouchsafed to us about his Indian background; its honesty and superiority is assumed and considered to be beyond question. When eventually he finds himself a lonely, brooding figure in a decaying pioneer community, he serves dramatically as an unimpeachable moral centre from which the film judges, and ultimately condemns, his white companions. In some ways he embodies Norman Mailer's concept of the 'White Negro', and inevitably he has to die.

Hombre is an extraordinary landmark in the development of the Western. An equally pronounced example, and a rather comic one, of the way attitudes towards Indians have changed over the past couple of decades is found in comparing Shelley Winters' response to the same situation in Mann's *Winchester '73* (1950) and Sydney Pollack's *The Scalphunters* (1968). In the earlier film she is a young pioneer wife trapped with a cavalry patrol by an Indian war party. As the Indians prepare for their final assault, James Stewart slips her a gun. Contemplating a fate worse than death, she nods in stoic recognition, and referring to the final bullet, she says, 'I understand about the last one.' As a blousy, big-hearted whore in *The Scalphunters*, she quite happily quits the company of uncouth, ill-smelling outlaws with whom she has been travelling, to go off with her handsome Kiowa captors. 'What the hell, they're only men,' she shrugs and reflects that the Indian chief is going to get 'the damnedest white squaw in the Kiowa nation'.

Implicit in many of these pictures is a rejection of the view that Indians are a deadly menace and that their culture is too alien to live with. From this position it is a relatively short move towards seeing what can be learned from them, and only another step to seeing them as an alternative, or counter, culture. This was proposed back in 1956 in Samuel Fuller's didactic *Run of the Arrow*, which centres upon an Irish-Southerner (Rod Steiger) who fires the last shot at Appomattox and, refusing to become accommodated to post-Civil War life, goes West to undergo the painful initiation which will make him a full member of the Sioux nation. Reluctantly he is won back to white civilisation by a Northern cavalry officer who gives him a glib lesson in American history, and the picture concludes with the admonitory title (replacing 'The End'), 'The End of this story can only be written by you.' It is characteristic of Fuller, incidentally, that at one stage he identifies the troublesome young Sioux braves with present-day American juvenile delinquents.

Run of the Arrow anticipated by a decade several of the most ambitious works of the past few years and a social trend among the young which has led to books on Indian history filling the avant-garde bookshops from San Francisco to St Germain-des-Prés. In the theatre we have seen Arthur Kopits' play *Indians* (1968), and in the cinema Elliot Silverstein's *A Man Called Horse* (1970), Ralph Nelson's *Soldier Blue* (1970) and Arthur Penn's *Little Big Man* (1970). Each of these films, in their varying ways, presents Indian life as a valid counter culture, a more organic, life-enhancing existence than white society, from which the central character in each film gains a new perspective on society and a new humanity. In *A Man Called Horse*, he is an English nobleman (Richard Harris), revitalised by a peculiarly gruelling sojourn among the Sioux; in *Soldier Blue*, an American girl (Candice Bergen) becomes an incredibly articulate critic of her culture (as well as an unbelievably foul-mouthed one) after her period of captivity among the

89

'A peculiarly gruelling sojourn among the Sioux': Richard Harris initiated in *A Man Called Horse*

Cheyenne; in *Little Big Man*, a picaresque hero (Dustin Hoffman) drifts back and forth between his adoptive Cheyenne family and a corrupt white frontier society. All three films are less inhibited in their acknowledgment of the brutal aspects of Indian life than the earlier liberal movies which argued a case for mutual respect, tolerance and peaceable relations.

Indicative of their closeness to contemporary concerns is the fact that both *Soldier Blue* and *Little Big Man* offer direct parallels with the Vietnam situation, and perhaps even with My Lai, in their presentation of cavalry massacres and the deliberate policy of exterminating Indians. The climax of *Soldier Blue* is a reconstruction of the Sand Creek Massacre, which is updated from 1864 to 1876 to place it the year after Custer's defeat at Little Big Horn. *Little Big Man* has at its centre a quite dazzling re-creation of the Washita River Massacre of 1866. Both are unsparing in their fashionable attacks on white vilisation', which they see as hypocritical, barbarous and ath-seeking. There are token 'good whites', to be sure, but the ntral thrust is directed against the ideology and behaviour of a ole society. (*Soldier Blue* handles the material with bludg-ning crudity, *Little Big Man* with feeling and subtlety, but e general drift is much the same.) In the introductory quence to *Little Big Man*, in which the 121-year-old narrator encouraged to reminisce by a present-day historian, the term nocide' is openly used to characterise the nineteenth-century atment of the Indians.

This contemporary framework makes possible what a few evious pictures have only been able to imply. In Richard ooks' forceful *The Last Hunt* (1955), for example, we had a thological Indian hater (Robert Taylor) bent on exterminat-g the remaining herds of bison. 'One less buffalo,' he says, eans one less Indian.' *The Last Hunt*, a box-office disaster in day, would no doubt be welcomed now as a significant ological Western.* Again, in John Ford's *Cheyenne Autumn* 964), there is a clear comparison made between the per-cution of the Indians and the German extermination camps in e performance of Karl Malden as Captain Wessels, a rigid uton just doing his duty as commandant of a grisly prison in nich the remnant of a decimated Cheyenne tribe is briefly carcerated. But *Little Big Man* presents the issue directly as e shame of a whole society and its almost conscious policy.

Little Big Man also manages for the first time to give a ajor role in a big budget movie to an Indian actor in casting hief Dan George as Dustin Hoffman's Indian 'father', Old dge Skins. Previously, star Indian roles and even minor

---

* Long before the state of the environment became an international occupation, the Western took up the cause. The low-budget *Back in the ddle* (1941) is a pure ecological Western with Gene Autry fighting inst an evil mill-owner who is poisoning cattle by dumping copper hate into a river running through the valley and refuses to desist from anti-social activities.

'One less buffalo means one less Indian': Robert Taylor in Richard Brooks' *The L.*
Hunt

speaking parts of any importance have regularly been assign
to white actors; indeed it was only a chance last-minu
decision to cast Chief Dan George. The film also goes son
way towards finding a satisfactory dramatic language for tl
Indians, and Dan George manages to avoid that unctuo
solemnity of movie Indians. The result is not entirely satisfa
tory, but a move in the right direction. The alternative, I
suppose, is subtitles. In Raoul Walsh's *A Distant Trump*
(1964) and in Stuart Millar's *When the Legends Die* (197?
subtitles were used and they at least gave the Indians tl
dignity and respect which attaches to foreigners and tl
prestige of subtitled European movies; no one else has resort
to this except the makers of *Texas Across the River* (1967),
feeble comedy Western, one of the better touches of which w
to have the Indians speak in their native tongue and provi
unintelligible subtitles in Indian sign language.

le Big Man: Dustin Hoffman caught between the racial lines at Little Big
n

Little Big Man, with its beautifully realised evocation of
eyenne life, is perhaps the present highwater-mark in the
atment of Indians in the movies, as well as being a major
irical comment on the values and appeal of the Western
ire. Nevertheless, it is still open to the accusation of mani-
lating the Indians according to the political ideas and uncon-
ous cultural predilections of its makers. The charge has been
de that the Cheyenne in *Little Big Man* are less Indians than
w York Jews, and there is a good deal to be said for this
w. Indeed at the end, when Old Lodge Skins fails to bring
out his ritual, ceremonial death on a hilltop outside his
lage, he stands up, dusts himself down, and stoically
serves: 'Well, sometimes the magic works and sometimes it
esn't.' We should of course remember that it was the belief of
seph Smith and the Mormons that the Indians were in fact
wish, the descendants of the lost Hebrew tribes.

93

Two shades of black: Sidney Poitier in his own *Buck and the Preacher* . . .

Considering that probably 25 to 30 per cent of working co
boys in the nineteenth-century West were Negroes, the absen
of black faces during the seventy years of the Western's histc
is another case of Hollywood's failure to accord the countr
black minority an adequate, or even token, representation
the American cinema, beyond acknowledging their presen
as house servants. Not only has the Western traditiona
been devoted to upholding White Anglo-Saxon Protesta
supremacy – which has involved virtually all minorities, not ju
blacks, appearing in supporting and frequently comic roles – b
it has also tended to favour Southerners. Admittedly a lar
part of the transient labouring force in the West was made
of ex-Confederate soldiers, yet to an unusual degree, both
Civil War movies (from *Birth of a Nation* through *Gone W
the Wind*) and in post-Civil War Westerns, Hollywood h
tended to be an apologist for the South and to locate in t
dispossessed Southerner the ideal of the chivalrous cowboy.

. and in Ralph Nelson's *Duel at Diablo*

In the Thirties and Forties, according to Fenin and Everson, there were apparently a number of low-budget horse operas featuring black actors made strictly for ghetto audiences in America and never shown abroad. Predictably, in the Seventies the sudden realisation that a profitable black audience exists again for rather more elaborate specialist fare has led to something of a revival, with such black Westerns as Sidney Poitier's *Buck and the Preacher* (1972) and *The Legend of Nigger Charley* (1972). Where this unpromising start will lead remains to be seen.

As I have previously remarked, the Indian has often been a surrogate Negro in numerous liberal Westerns of the 1950s, at a time when Hollywood was soft-pedalling in the area of contemporary social conscience movies, immediately following the brief rash of pictures about black-white relations (*Pinky*, *Lost Boundaries* and *Home of the Brave* all appeared in 1949); and this may have been of some slight consolation to Negro

audiences, who are said to have identified in the past wit
Indians.

One of the obvious explanations for the presence of isolate
black characters in recent Westerns has been the need t
provide roles in the most enduringly popular of genres fc
prominent black actors, such as Sidney Poitier as the coo
cynical cavalry horsebreaker in Ralph Nelson's *Duel at Diab*
(1965) and Sammy Davis Jr in the feeble Sinatra Clan rom
Sergeants Three (1962), a Western remake of *Gunga D*
which gave Davis the opportunity to play Kipling's regiment:
bisti as a cavalry bugler.

A rather more rewarding role went to Ossie Davis in *Th
Scalphunters* (1968), a robust semi-comedy of impeccabl
liberal attitudes, where he plays an escaped slave of great soci:
sophistication who puts to shame the uncouth, illiterat
Westerners among whom he unhappily lands on his way t
freedom in Mexico in the 1850s. He insists that he is
Comanche who has learned his fine ways through an assoc
ation with an educated family in the South, but he become
an object of trade and bargaining between both Whites an
Indians. Typical of the film's somewhat embarrassing goo
intentions is a fight in a pool between Davis and Burt Lancaste
which leaves both so caked in mud as to be racially indistir
guishable.

Several films have presented units of black cavalrymen. Th
best of them is Robert Parrish's *The Wonderful Countr*
(1959), where their role is marginal; the most significant i
John Ford's *Sergeant Rutledge* (1960). Unfortunately Ford'
film is gravely weakened by having as its dramatic structure a
indifferent Perry Mason-style courtroom drama in which th
almost saintly eponymous hero (Woody Strode) is wrongl
standing trial for rape and murder. In handling this court
martial aspect, Ford is at his most embarrassingly self
indulgent, and one suspects that it held little interest for him
What he is interested in doing, and does well, is to present hi

(*left*) Black as Fordian hero: Woody Strode in *Sergeant Rutledge*. (*right*) *Invitation to a Gunfighter:* Yul Brynner as Jules Gaspard d'Estaing

black cavalrymen in precisely the same heroic manner that he earlier used for their white counterparts – silhouetted against the horizon, trekking through the desert, making dignified compositions of the statuesque Strode against sharply rising buttes. 'It's all right for Mr Lincoln to say we're free, but we're not free yet,' is the theme, and Ford wishes to give his black soldiers their due place in American history. 'The 9th Cavalry was my home, my freedom,' says Rutledge, and addressing his men he insists that 'the 9th's record is going to speak for us all one day and it's going to speak clean.' Sadly the film does not rank high in the great director's work, but it is touching to see him, after so many years of patronising black performers, confer on them one of the greatest gifts at his disposal, which is to make them full citizens of his beloved Monument Valley.

Woody Strode has also made other less celebrated excursions into the West – as an Indian in Ford's *Two Rode*

the lamentable British Western *Shalako*, and as a
hunter and ace bowman, hired as one of *The
(1966) to join Robert Ryan, Lee Marvin and
r on their expedition into revolutionary Mexico.
ade of his colour here; everything centres on his
s. Both of these elements, however, are central to
nce of another top black athlete-turned-actor, Jim
e two Westerns which take him into Mexico – *Rio*
1964) and *100 Rifles* (1968). The first is a most
g picture which inexorably builds to an apocalyptic
which Brown, as a cavalry sergeant, and Richard
, as a surly Indian-hating racist Southerner, perish
ther in destroying a consignment of stolen weapons which
s fallen into the hands of renegade Indians and their ex-
Confederate allies. In *100 Rifles* Brown figures as an American
mercenary assisting Mexican revolutionaries (his political in-
volvement has obvious contemporary parallels), and enjoys the
sexual favours of Miss Raquel Welch. It could be argued that
the acceptance of the once taboo subject of miscegenation has
been gradually prepared for through the relationships between
white frontiersmen and Indian women, though the latter (e.g
Debra Paget in *Broken Arrow*, Dolores del Rio in *Flaming
Star*, Elsa Martinelli in *The Indian Fighter*, Audrey Hepburn
in *The Unforgiven*) were all played by white actresses.

Western examples are naturally to be found of that favourite
American and Hollywood activity – the lifting of the lid from a
seemingly ordinary community to expose the seething vice
nastiness and racialism underneath. The pursuit is a laudable
one, but as often in the Western the result can prove disturb
ingly anachronistic, making the audience only too well aware
that attitudes widely accepted in their time are being exposed as
egregious excesses. In *Invitation to a Gunfighter* the task of
exposure falls to a sophisticated octoroon from New Orleans
played by Yul Brynner, who gives the community a lesson in
tolerance, as well as teaching the ignorant townsfolk how to

pronounce his distinguished French name (Jules Gaspard d'Estaing), before perishing rather than kill the man they have hired him to kill, who happens to be a Confederate soldier lately returned from losing the Civil War. In *Death of a Gunfighter* (1969) the task of instruction falls to an ageing, unwanted sheriff (Richard Widmark), and before dying at the hands of his anti-semitic, anti-Mexican, antipathetic employers, his last act is to marry his mistress, the proprietress of the local saloon and brothel, played by the black singer Lena Horne. The part of the town's leading bigot and organiser of the sheriff's downfall is taken by Carrol O'Connor, later to make his name as Archie Bunker in *All in the Family*, the American television version of *Till Death Us Do Part*.

4: Landscape, Violence, Poker

If not from the start, when *Cripple Creek Bar-room* (1898) was shot in the Edison Studio and *The Great Train Robbery* filmed on location in New Jersey, at least from quite early days the landscape has been an integral part of the Western both as an ingredient in the genre's popular appeal and for its role in shaping the dramatic action. Frequently the landscape is simply there to be admired, which is not unacceptable. The American West has an intrinsic beauty worth recording for its own sake, as witness the work of painters, and later photographers, from colonial times to the present.

And the land is not only beautiful and awe-inspiring but possessed of strange surrealist qualities: Max Ernst was struck by the close resemblance between the imaginary landscape he dreamt up for his study of the destruction and renewal of life, *Europe After the Rain*, when he began his large CinemaScope shaped canvas in 1940, and the real landscape of Arizona which he first saw during his American exile when he was halfway towards completing it. One of the most haunting Western scenes I know is to be found in Gordon Douglas' *Rio Conchos* (1964), where a deranged ex-Confederate colonel has established the headquarters of his band of marauders on a hill above a Mexican river in a half-built mansion; through the windows of the palladian façade one can see the sky – and it looks like, has the same disturbing qualities of, a Magritte.

The two most important native-born artists of the so-called Abstract Expressionist school, Adolph Gottlieb (born New York, 1903) and Jackson Pollock (born on a ranch near Cody, Wyoming, in 1912) were deeply influenced by the West. A turning point in Gottlieb's development came in 1937 when he spent a year in the desert outside Tucson, Arizona, during which time he assimilated aspects of the local landscape and Indian art while casting off the European shackles he had so happily taken on in his youth. Look at, say, Boetticher's *Ride Lonesome* or Hellman's *The Shooting* – the burning sand, the oppressive sky, the fractured, enigmatic shards of civilisation which litter the desolate terrain – look at them abstractly and you see and *feel* the world which helped shape the mature Gottlieb style and provided him with a personal iconography.

Pollock spent his formative years drifting around Arizona in the 1920s, from the Mexican border to the southern rim of the Grand Canyon, in the company of rough itinerant labourers. His biographer B. H. Friedman writes of the popular European image of Pollock as 'a hard-riding hard-drinking cowboy from the Wild West who came roaring, maybe even shooting, his way into New York where he took the art galleries by storm.'* This is an expression of that conventional rhetoric of American life and the foreign response to it I have spoken of earlier, by

---

* *Jackson Pollock* (Weidenfeld and Nicolson, London, 1973), p. 3. I find it interesting that three notable American artists of the post-Abstract Expressionist period – Jasper Johns, Kenneth Noland and Frank Stella, each representing quite different schools – should have lent Navajo blankets from their personal collections to the celebrated exhibition which toured America and Europe in 1972–3. There is no suggestion that North American Indian art significantly influenced their work – on the contrary, it was their paintings which helped fellow-countrymen to recognise the aesthetic value, admittedly divorced from the complex culture that produced them, of these extraordinary artifacts. But Navajo blankets and rugs – as well as the deliberately ephemeral art of sand-painting – arise from the Western terrain and light, and are part of the shared experience discussed here.

Personal landscape: John Ford's Monument Valley (*Stagecoach*) ▶

which Henry Kissinger went into the last stages of the Vietnam peace talks in Paris identifying (ingratiating?) himself to the press as a wary gunfighter coming into town, to clear up the mess created by Lyndon Johnson, who once provoked Charles de Gaulle to say (according to his biographer Pierre Galante) 'He's a cowboy . . . born in the land of the ranch and the Colt who shot his way up to sheriff.' Pollock was of course influenced by the frontier company he kept in his youth, but his art is more closely related to the West than Friedman's jocular gloss on his life-style conveys. Like Gottlieb, he too was immensely affected, as Friedman goes on to suggest, by the overwhelming landscape, the strange qualities of light, the Indian pictographs, and by, I think one can fairly say, the tragic sense and desperate challenge of the West.

The Western movie, like the best Western art, is naturally most effective when it goes beyond the merely picturesque. Certain directors have established their personal landscape in the West. The most notable and best known is John Ford's Monument Valley, straddling Arizona and Utah in the Navajo Reservation with its cathedral-like buttes and mesas rising out of the flat red desert, where eight of Ford's thirteen sound Westerns have been made. The terrain may not always have been suitable to the stated geographical location of the subjects, for Monument Valley is a unique and relatively small area; but it provided him with what is universally regarded as his own moral universe, which he has rendered so powerfully that a visitor to Monument Valley is overwhelmed by recollection of Ford movies. Other directors too have created their own worlds, especially Budd Boetticher and Anthony Mann. Boetticher's arid corner of the South West, with its smooth clusters of rock like Easter Island statues which have had their features rubbed away, is the perfect setting for his series of severe little fables starring Randolph Scott; verdant oases occur in his films as interludes for contemplation and sometimes (most notably the showdown in *Ride Lonesome*) for thematic resolution. The

...ndscape for thematic resolution: Boetticher's *Ride Lonesome*

...verse is the case with Anthony Mann, who for the most part ...vours lush prairie and beautiful hill country and tends to ...serve denuded or snow-covered settings for his most severe ...amatic statements.

In his study of the formative years of American culture, *O ...range New World*, Howard Mumford Jones lists five 'signifi- ...nt components in the delineation of the Western landscape ...paint and words': astonishment, plenitude, vastness, in- ...ngruity and melancholy.* All these are present in varying ...grees whenever a camera is turned upon the American land- ...ape. And they play a part in producing, as well as helping to ...aracterise, what John W. McCoubrey, in a fascinating and ...ovocative book, has called *The American Tradition in ...inting.*† What Dr McCoubrey has to say about American art

* *O Strange New World: American Culture: The Formative Years* ...hatto and Windus, London, 1965), p. 379.
† George Braziller, New York, 1963.

from colonial days to the present has a great bearing on t
American cinema in general and the Western in particular:

Our art is possessed by the spaciousness and emptiness of the la
itself. No American painter can ignore it; to make its presence felt
his work, he has consciously avoided, or never needed, these ski
which traditionally bottle up, control or make habitable pictori
space ... Thus figures in American paintings – like their viewers
are not given an easy mastery of the space they occupy. Rather, th
stand in tentative relation to it, without any illusion of command ov
it.

And in comparing a European abstract painting by Soulage
which is tightly constructed and wholly contained within t
canvas, with a superficially similar one by the American Fra
Kline, he observes that the violent brush strokes in the latt
'as they reach to the very edges of the canvas – and seeming
beyond – imply the continuation of vast distances, the presen
of an enormous void, of which the area of the painting is bu
fragment.'

The location of the Westerner in his landscape is a matter
paramount importance, and there are relatively few movi
which do not begin with the single man or group of men ridi
through the countryside. This is even true of those pictur
largely set in towns where the sense of space is implied – as
the Kline painting *Crosstown* referred to by McCoubrey –
the dusty streets reaching out to the limitless surroundi
tracts, a feeling evoked by shots down the main street in *R
Bravo* and by the railroad disappearing in the heat haze
High Noon. Both *Rio Bravo* and *High Noon* are prefaced
people riding into town – in each case these are visitors and n
the marshals, for were it to be otherwise, the resident lawm
played by Wayne and Cooper would be detached from t
communities which they embody. In another town-centr
Western, *The Gunfighter*, the person we see crossing the des
at the beginning, indeed almost the only person we see ridi

106

one in the countryside at any time, is Gregory Peck as the
doomed gunslinger, the man on the move whose arrival is a
sure sign of disruption in the community.

This contrast between open land and the town, between the
illusion of freedom and the necessity of compromise, between a
relaxed association with nature and a tense accommodation to
society, lies at the roots of the genre. Certainly the mood of a
western is established at the outset by the way directors place
their protagonists in relationship to the surroundings, and over
the past twenty-odd years the approach to the question has
become increasingly self-conscious. The way the detached,
buckskin-clad Alan Ladd almost floated down out of the mountains in *Shane* could scarcely be more calculated. The same is
true of the opening of Don Siegel's *Two Mules for Sister Sara*
(1969), a succession of panning shots from various animals (an
owl, a fish, a rabbit, a mountain lion, a snake, a tarantula) over
to Clint Eastwood as he rides confidently through the beautiful,
unspoilt Mexican terrain. We take the film-maker's point that
the man is himself a wild animal very much at home in the
country; but after a few shots we begin to become conscious of
their calculation, full of the same kind of admiration for the
cameraman's skill and patience that we feel when seeing a
clever nature film like Disney's *Living Desert*.

Admittedly the aestheticised mood is built up only to be
deliberately broken by Eastwood's horse crushing the last
example of the local fauna, the tarantula. Nothing, we are made
to feel, can stop this arrogant man – and we are right. How
superficially similar and yet how different is the opening of *The
Wild Bunch*. Here the outlaw band, their immaculate military
disguise and steady riding pace placing them in such a confidently superior position to the demented pedestrians involved
in a revival meeting, enter a Texas border town to stage their
holdup. Far from treading on tarantulas, the group's fate is
prefigured by their identification with a couple of poisonous
scorpions fed into a tray of ants and burned by a crowd of

callous children: 'As flies to wanton boys are we to the God
they kill us for their sport.'

A contrast of another kind would be with the openin
of Arthur Penn's *The Left-Handed Gun* (1958), Hen
Hathaway's *From Hell to Texas* (1958) and Peckinpah's *T
Ballad of Cable Hogue* (1970), which stress the vulnerability
their heroes by presenting them without, or rapidly dispo
sessed of, their horses, and facing a remorseless land,
situation which prepares us for the moral and drama
evolution of their heroes in a very different way from Siegel

The allegorical journey where the land itself seems to dete
mine and reflect the film's dramatic development is a comm
enough phenomenon and never more perfectly realised than
Anthony Mann's last important Western, *Man of the We*
(1958) – perhaps his finest, and certainly his most pessimist
movie. The film begins with a reformed outlaw, Link Jon
(Gary Cooper), warily entering an unfamiliar town to make
train journey, the object of which is to hire a schoolteacher f
the remote Texas community in which he lives. He is thus
man already redeemed and accommodated to settled way
unlike the heroes of earlier Mann Westerns. But the implicati
of the movie is that he has merely broken with the past, set
aside, has not exorcised it. The train is attacked by band
and he is stranded with a saloon singer and an unsuccess
gambler. Suspecting that his old gang was responsible for t
hold-up, he leads his two companions to the only shelter
knows in the vicinity, an abandoned farmhouse where, su
enough, the gang is waiting, led by the insane Dock Tobin (L
J. Cobb) and his sons, who are in effect the only family t
younger Link had ever known.

Returning to this parody of a homestead and caricature o
family, standing amid hospitable green countryside which
one farms and on which no cattle graze, Link is forced
accompany the Tobin gang on their last big job – the robbe
of the bulging bank at the mining town of Lasso – before th

ad across the border into Mexican exile. As they progress,
 atmosphere becomes increasingly tense, Tobin's behaviour
r more erratic; habitable land gives way to desert as they
ve further away from civilisation, culminating in the
covery that Lasso is now a dry, decaying ghost town.
asso' suggests a trap and a noose, just as 'Link' has the
vious dual significance of a name drawn from Abe Lincoln
d the implication of a figure standing between the settled and
 primitively atavistic.) Here Link must make his final settle-
nt with his 'brothers' and his insane surrogate father,
ose last destructive act is to rape the captive saloon girl.
an of the West has its longueurs, but few Westerns can match
 integration of setting, dramatic development and moral
ogress.

Mann's use of the ghost town was of course by no means
w, and indeed it is among the Western's most compelling
tings. The genre seems happier with it than with an estab-
hed community. Most Western towns bigger than a handful
 isolated buildings lack a sense of on-going life. They seem
pulated by extras shuffling uneasily around on purposeless
rands, waiting to take their place as spectators in some
minent dramatic confrontation. This uneasiness is employed
 good effect in *Monte Walsh*, when a pair of old cowhands,
wly arrived in town, ask a ranch foreman the question every-
e has been dying to ask for years – why are all these people
nging around doing nothing? 'They're out of work,' is the
onic reply.

At any rate the ghost town as the objective correlative of the
permanence of American life, a pessimistic feeling about the
gility of American civilisation and its problems in putting
wn roots, is a forceful image. Like *Man of the West*,
merous Westerns involve an inexorable journey towards a
ost town where the central characters are doomed to die or
erge shriven. At a conventional level we see this in Andrew
cLaglen's *Bandolero!* (1968), where two brothers, reunited

109

'The impermanence of American life': the abandoned mining camp in *The Law o*
Jake Wade

in crime, perish together and are buried side by side in
deserted Mexican adobe village, when they might have used t
proceeds of a robbery to buy a ranch in Montana. In a mc
complex vein, the journey of self-discovery in Peckinpah's fil
movie, *The Deadly Companions*, is to a ghost town where t
heroine can bury her dead son by her late husband, and the
accompanying her can dispense with an unseen Apache dc
ging their trail and settle a blood feud left over from the Ci
War. Likewise in John Sturges' best Western, *The Law a*
Jake Wade (1958), the last third of the picture is set in
abandoned mining camp, where buried in the graveyard is t
loot which binds a reformed outlaw to his old gang. Odd
enough, Alfred Hitchcock's first thriller with an Americ
setting, *Saboteur* (1942), took him briefly into a ghost tow
And less oddly Joseph Losey, whose American career was c
short before he had the opportunity of making the Western

rue Grit: jousting knights

lanned, chose a ghost town as the location for the final
equence of *The Prowler* (1950), using it as the ultimate place
f retreat for his pathetic, fugitive cop as his dreams of success
nd social acceptance crumble to dust.

The ghost town inevitably imposes certain attitudes upon the
iewer. The open country on the other hand, as I have implied, is
ubject to being manipulated to suit the film-maker's purpose.
he magnificence of the landscape can be used to aggrandise
he action — to elevate the activities of the Westerner into
)lympian encounters which derive a heroic purity and detach-
nent from the surroundings. This is the way the showdown
etween the one-eyed bounty-hunter (John Wayne) and a band
f ugly desperadoes works in *True Grit* — as they ride towards
ach other across a clearing in the forest, the scene takes on the
spect of a joust between medieval knights. Whereas in Dick
Richards' *Culpepper Cattle Company* we are constantly aware

111

of the discrepancy between the magnificent scenery and th
squalid events enacted within it and the sordid little commur
ities emplanted upon it.

If I have given the impression that the visual aspect of th
Western is largely a matter of the direct confrontation betwee
the film-maker and the landscape, I must qualify this in severa
ways. No one today can easily bring a totally fresh, primitiv
eye to the land. The traditions of American art, of photo
graphy, of the Western genre itself, interpose themselves. O
occasion these traditions are consciously present, as when
cinematographer bases his style on Western artists lik
Remington and Russell, or on pioneer photographers. Tha
'authentic' Civil War look of John Huston's *The Red Badge c
Courage* derives from a close study of Matthew Brady's pic
tures, and films like *High Noon* and Delmer Daves' *3.10 t
Yuma* seem clearly to have aimed at a gritty, grainy qualit
intended to evoke nineteenth-century photographs. *Butc
Cassidy and the Sundance Kid* also uses the style of contem
porary photographers, but in an altogether more showy way. .
Man Called Horse* would seem to have drawn upon earlie
Western painters of Indian life such as George Catlin, Alfre
Miller and Karl Bodmer for its compositions and colou
values. In several pictures set in Mexico one can detect th
influence of Mexican paintings, particularly those of River
and Orozco, with their stylised groupings of peasants an
revolutionaries. One sees this in the hieratic arrangement c
the importunate peons in the face of their American saviour
in *The Magnificent Seven*. Here their position is subservien
More often it is heroic, as in the endless lines of identica
white-clad, sombrero-topped Juaristas who appear on th
skylines or the battlements to look down on the America
mercenaries in Robert Aldrich's equally studied *Vera Cru
(1954). In both cases the contrast is between th
individualised Americans and the anonymous, collectiv
mass of the Mexicans.

112

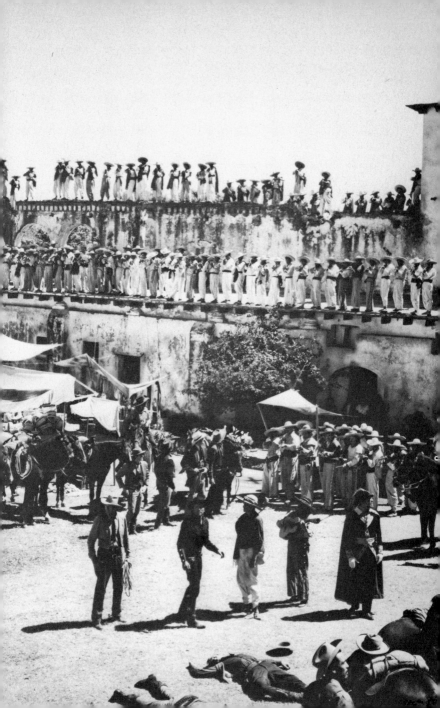

'Violence,' said the Black Power ideologue Rap Brown, 'is as American as cherry pie'; and a non-violent Western is as odd as unthinkable, as a vegetarian steakhouse. In the past twenty years, however, a good many Westerns have tended to be exceedingly selfconscious about the way they earn their bread and butter. They have preached sermons against violence, while benefiting from, or exulting in, violence. Depending upon the direction from which one approaches the subject, this could be called a central contradiction of the genre or simple hypocrisy Apologists for the Western's traditionally healthy cathartic qualities have been troubled by the discomforting violence in movies which – this disturbing element aside – they would tend to approve of. Yet the simple fact is that the more seriously violence is taken by the film-maker, the more likely its expression will be to break the accepted entertainment conventions – shocking the audience and offending the susceptibilities of liberal critics.

Consequently, the traditional approach adopted by the Goldwater school will seem controlled, ritualised, acceptable while the sharper, more realistic depiction of similar events in the Kennedy Western might seem disturbing and, on superficial examination, morbid or even sadistic.* In what I must call the more serious Westerns, the quantity of violence has diminished and its quality become altogether more intense. In Martin Ritt's *Hombre*, for example, there is a single violent incident in the first half-hour, when the hero employs a rifle-butt to strike the face of a cowboy who has been taunting some Indians in an all-

---

* I have written elsewhere on the history and the social and aesthetic problems of violence in the cinema, and I am here restricting myself to violence in the Western. My essay 'Violence in the Movies', written originally for *Twentieth Century* (Winter, 1964–5), is reprinted in *Sight Sound and Society*, edited by David Manning White and Richard Averson (Beacon Press, Boston, 1968) and *Violence in the Mass Media*, edited by Otto Larsen (Harper and Row, New York, 1969).

white saloon. The effect is literally shattering, for the victim is holding a glass to his lips, but the duration is about two seconds. In Boetticher's *Tall T* there is a mood of incipient violence throughout, carefully cued by social and domestic events, which wells up and quickly subsides as Randolph Scott despatches his three captors one by one, using methods which relate existential circumstance to individual come-uppance and calculated (morally and aesthetically) to give them their just deserts. Incipient violence, too, determines the structure of *High Noon*. As the clock ticks inexorably towards the final encounter, the actual scenes of physical confrontation – one fistfight, one shootout – occupy about five minutes of the picture. This very sparing use of action is dramatically admirable, and possibly socially responsible, yet it has the effect perhaps – as does the dull forty minutes of initial scene-setting in Hitchcock's *The Birds* – of almost making the audience *will* the violence upon the characters involved. It can also lead to over-emphasis on the purely aesthetic, virtuoso, aspects of staging gunfights.

The tone of fistfights is usually a key to a film's approach to violence. In the Johnson and Goldwater-style films of John Ford and his natural successor Andrew V. McLaglen, these fights are hardly ever taken seriously. They are usually conducted between comrades and friendly rivals. Davy Crockett's followers engage in fisticuffs for fun in *The Alamo*; John Wayne and his brothers bust up the family home in *The Sons of Katie Elder*. Often a fight involves dozens of people, like the punch-up in *McLintock!* or the vast post-Civil War brawl between Northerners and Southerners on the Fourth of July in McLaglen's *The Undefeated*. The result of a hundred punches, shattered chairs, broken saloon mirrors, fractured bannisters and falling chandeliers will at the most be a few bruises, a couple of black eyes and the odd piece of sticking plaster. The bartender has ducked, and the pianist has gone into a frenzied rendition of 'Buffalo Girls' to accompany a playful ritual which

'The camera edges in close on their brutal contests': violence in Anthony Mann's *The Man From Laramie*

can often be as stylised, graceful and artfully choreographed as a ballet.

There is something here which reflects the rough-and-tumble of frontier life: this is actually framed within William Fraker's *Monte Walsh*, when some old cowhands nearly wreck their bunkhouse in a tough, friendly brawl, and end up laughing, sensing that they've caught a little of the old departed spirit, declaring that they haven't enjoyed themselves so much in months. They have, of course, been behaving like children, getting something out of their system, as a knowing glance from the ranch boss (representing the new, anonymous, commercial 'system' itself) indicates. An observer of the scene in another attempt at a realistic depiction of Western life, *Will Penny*, looks at the irresponsible behaviour of cowboys and notes just that: 'Children – dangerous children.'

At the far end of the spectrum from the expansive brawling

The futility of violence: Gregory Peck and Charlton Heston in William Wyler's *The Big Country*

of John Wayne in Goldwater and Johnson movies, there are the Westerns of Anthony Mann, where fistfights have even greater intensity than shootouts. In *Winchester '73* and *The Man From Laramie*, James Stewart and his opponents sweat, grunt, get really battered, and the camera edges in close on their brutal contests. The fights invariably end with someone getting badly hurt, and in the case of Gary Cooper taking on a ruthless opponent in *Man of the West*, two people get killed, one of them an innocent bystander. Here the dialectic of the Western is at work, forming a bond within a society or destroying it, and both themes have their validity. Somewhere between the extremes of the Mann approach to fistfights and that of the John Ford school is the partly satirical marathon scrap between Eastern seafarer Gregory Peck and ranch foreman Charlton Heston in *The Big Country*, which is presented in long shot in the moonlight and continues until both men are down on their knees exhausted. The complex brawl in the present-day Prescott bar at rodeo-time in Peckinpah's *Junior Bonner* draws on these established conventions – as understood both by the participants and a suitably conditioned worldwide audience – and enables the eponymous hero to provoke the disturbance and yet maintain his heroic stance while sensibly withdrawing from the subsequent mêlée.

If it is true that Westerns most opposed to violence turn out to be the most violent, it is perhaps also true that they are likely to evidence a strong vein of masochism. Mann's heroes are frequently wounded in painful ways which go far beyond the obvious purpose of providing a revenge motive. In his two Westerns (and in several of his other films) Marlon Brando undergoes extreme degradation at the hands of sadistic enemies. In each case the emphasis falls on his pain rather than his tormentors' pleasure. These symbolic wounds of course place the Westerner in a much older tradition of the mythic hero. And the recurrent ritual of removing bullets or arrows from the hero's body (a process drawn out to inordinate lengths in Don Siegel's *Two Mules for Sister Sara*) suggests that the aim is principally a test of manhood, of the ability to endure pain without flinching, rather than simply the punishment of the protagonist.

Having said all this, I must nevertheless reiterate that for film-makers and moviegoers alike the staging and viewing of violent spectacles are among the genre's prime attractions. Where this is the only motive – as it seems to be in most Italian Westerns – there is perhaps cause for censure. Yet such moral judgments are not easily arrived at. A case in point is a recent preoccupation with the gallows and the business of hanging.

Certain crude movies of the Fifties which most critics roundly condemned – *The Hangman* (1959) and *Good Day for a Hanging* (1959) – led to the multiple legal executions shown in *Hang 'Em High*, *Bandolero!* and *True Grit*. The executions in *True Grit* might be explained away as the presentation of the

118

The Western remains firmly committed to capital punishment': *Hang 'Em High*

...rue facts of frontier life and even their brutalising effects on ...he young, and intermittently in that picture there is a vein of ...black humour which informs the opening section of *Bandolero!*, ...n which James Stewart poses as a public hangman to free his ...brother's gang, and turns the notion of gallows humour into ...rope-and-timber reality. There is, however, in both films a mor- ...bid streak which colours the whole of *Hang 'Em High*, where ...he central relationship is between a law enforcement officer ...and a self-righteous 'hanging judge' based on the celebrated ...saac Charles Parker of Arkansas Territory, a personal appoin- ...ee of President Grant. John Huston's *The Life and Times of ...Judge Roy Bean* (1972) also exploits the darkly comic aspects ...of hanging, to dubious effect. There are undoubtedly reflections ...of the time here, but whatever way one cares to look at the ...matter, the Western – for all its constant preaching against ...ynch law – remains firmly committed to capital punishment. ...One could argue that for it to be otherwise would be a gross

119

falsification of history. It is at such moments that one recalls a Western of a more conventionally liberal cast, Raoul Walsh' *The Tall Men* (1955), which opens with Clark Gable and Cameron Mitchell riding towards a corpse hanging from a tree 'Looks like we're near civilisation,' says Gable.

The trouble with Western violence lies not with the inflexibility of the genre's metaphor or the audience's ability to interpret it, but with its immutability. At the end of Preminger' *River of No Return*, a little boy shoots his father's would-be killer in the back, thereby learning from experience how his father could once have done the same thing, been dubbed coward and sent to jail. *Day of the Evil Gun* concludes with Glenn Ford exchanging his pistols for clothes and having his life saved when the storekeeper uses the gun against Ford' treacherous partner. Johnny Ringo in *The Gunfighter* lies dying, aware that his young killer will now carry the deadly curse of being the fastest gun around. The doomed outlaws in *The Wild Bunch* know that their way of life has come to an end, that they cannot change, and join together in a final confrontation which they cannot possibly survive. These are general and intelligible statements about life, of varying degree of validity and complexity. One can duplicate them endlessly in a hundred other Westerns. But in each case a man, or several men, lies dead in the street. This is the murderous algebra of the Western and its ultimate limitation. The same argument on the other hand could be levelled against dramatic tragedy.

The most immediate and continuously topical accusation against the Western is the role it plays in sustaining an outdated and dangerous pattern of behaviour which not only encourages violence but, in lending assistance to the American gun lobby in its battle against legislation to control firearms, makes available the weapons which give lethal expression to that violent urge. 'The frontier myth is nonsense, literally bloody nonsense, because it can still excuse and glorify personal violence,' wrote Louis Heren, Washington correspondent of *The Times*, in the

...ake of the Robert Kennedy and Martin Luther King assassina-
...ons. And on the failure to enact effective laws to regulate
...rms, he remarked:

...he common excuse is the powerful lobby of the National Rifle
...ssociation, but I am not convinced. The main reason is the frontier
...yth, with its lonely hero triumphant in a hostile world, perpetuated
...ot only by films and television but by authors ranging from
...enimore Cooper and Ernest Hemingway to Mickey Spillane. It is
...out time Americans grew up.

...r Heren undoubtedly has a general point, but frankly I
...annot see the frontier myth as a particularly significant factor
...determining the actions of Sirhan Sirhan and James Earl
...ay – or for that matter Lee Harvey Oswald and Arthur
...remer.

...do not think it right to deal with violence in the Western
...ithout also mentioning the treatment of death. Death in cow-
...oy movies is not the euphemistic embalming process of Forest
...awn, a matter to be avoided and disguised. Death is con-
...onted directly as a fact of existence, possibly the ultimate fact,
...ot to be taken lightly nor to be viewed without perspective. It
...the great leveller uniting hunter and prey, part of a pattern
...hich completes a life but at the same time implies a sense of
...e continuity of generations within families and societies.

...To me the attitude towards ageing and death is one of the
...ost impressive characteristics of the Western, and sets the
...st examples of the genre, and many mediocre ones as well,
...art from gangster films or spy movies. The gangster dies
...oung and unmourned; his victims are fellow criminals or
...nocent bystanders. In spy pictures death is perfunctory,
...surd and often comic; nobody bothers to pick up the corpses
...d we are not invited to remember them. The fact that
...esterns have taken to depicting violent death in all its pain

The ritual of burial: *The Tall Men* (Clark Gable, Jane Russell, Robert Ryan, J Garcia)

and horror in no way alters my view. Good or bad, Westerner is entitled to a Christian burial and his passing marked. That life may be easily taken does not mean that it cheap and of no significance.

Scenes of dying and the rituals of burial on the plains or frontier cemeteries abound and constitute some of the m poignant sequences in the genre. This may well be a Victori hangover, and while the presentation of these scenes canr always be defended against the charge of sentimentality, th are usually far from being morbid. Moreover, there can be lit commercial pressure to include them; they arise naturally fro what is best in the morality of the form. The burial of Torr the murdered Southerner in *Shane*, of the stammering cowb killed in the cattle stampede of *Red River*, of the old Mexic shepherd in *The Appaloosa*, are deeply moving in their u affected simplicity. There is a feeling in these fairly typi

124

mples of the price paid for settling the land. Not surpris-
y, many Westerns end on elegiac scenes of burial or in
eteries – *True Grit*, *Bandolero!*, *The Magnificent Seven*. In
n's *The Naked Spur*, a bounty hunter (James Stewart)
nowledges the futility of his revenge quest and renounces
reward his dead quarry will bring him by unstrapping the
y from a horse and burying it before riding off to start a
life.

he corollary to this is a deep contempt for those who fail to
ect the ritual. The opening scene of *Rio Conchos*, in which
deranged Indian-hating Texan (Richard Boone) cold-
dedly shoots at distant Indians conducting a burial service
ing a dust storm, immediately establishes that he is beyond
moral pale; the end of *The Wild Bunch*, where the sordid
d of singing bounty-hunters head back to the Texas border
the valuable bodies of their outlawed prey strapped to
es, is the film's ultimate image of cosmic disgust. By con-
t, Peckinpah's next film, *The Ballad of Cable Hogue*,
cludes rather laboriously on the most elaborately photo-
phed and edited funeral sequence in the genre, signifying not
the death of a man but of a way of life.

here is, I think, nothing inconsistent between this respect
the correct rituals of burial and the mostly comic role
gned to the undertaker. The mortician is after all the man who
fits from the business, and his dual function is that of grimly
norous *memento mori* and cynical commercial counter-
nt to the central figures' tragic or disinterested activities.
hammering of coffin nails is a premonition of someone's
th: when the dishevelled Gary Cooper in *High Noon* drops
the barber's shop to be cleaned up, the barber tells the
in-maker in the back room to keep quiet, and Cooper
rms him on leaving that he can get back to the job. One of
bleak jokes in *Welcome to Hard Times* is to have the
ous symbolic killer murder the undertaker, as if to prove
he can banish death itself, and to despatch the hearse out of

Lily Langtry in Texas: Paul Newman in *The Life and Times of Judge Roy Bean*

town carrying the dead mortician. The stranger who retrie
the elegant vehicle is then forced by the sheriff to become
town's new undertaker.

There are some notable death scenes which are not attend
with the usual obsequies – these are private affairs signifying
individual rounding out his own life. One thinks here of J
McCrea in *Guns in the Afternoon* sending his friends away
he prepares to die; in a memorably composed shot he looks
to the distant sierras for the last time before leaning back
slumping dead, his head just outside the frame of the wi
screen. And we remember his earlier statement: 'All I wan
to enter my house justified.' One thinks, too, of Elvis Presley
Don Siegel's fine *Flaming Star*, riding off to die alone in
mountains as his Indian mother (Dolores Del Rio) had d
earlier when, having seen the 'flaming star' of death, she
walked off into the night.

126

e cultural poverty of American life outside the great urban
tres is a matter of fact and concern. The cultural poverty of
old frontier life, on the other hand, is rarely a matter which
rries Western film-makers. If anything they have tended,
omission, to exaggerate it. At times, some of the Western
ning towns of the nineteenth century could offer as
de a variety and a higher quality of entertainment than is
rrently provided in Las Vegas. Only a few pictures have
ggested this: the actress Lily Langtry visiting Texas, for
tance, in William Wyler's *The Westerner* (1940) and John
ston's *The Life and Times of Judge Roy Bean* (1972), or
Booth family touring their relatively high-quality
akespeare productions in Philip Dunne's *Prince of Players*
955). Mostly the movies have concentrated on more
turesque third-rate companies, like the one which makes
brief appearance in Ford's *My Darling Clementine*, a
upe so bad that its leader (Alan Mowbray) needs a
mpt from Doc Holliday in Hamlet's soliloquy; or the
eat Healy and Co.'s travelling theatre, starring Anthony
inn and Sophia Loren, whose vicissitudes out West are
armingly recorded in George Cukor's *Heller in Pink*
hts (1960).

At a domestic level, culture tends to be frowned upon,
arded as a women's concern and an Eastern frippery, which
not altogether misleading as a reflection of American
itudes. Some tentative approaches have been made towards
mining cultural activities as a status-seeking pursuit, but
the most part this aspect of life has been ignored.
casionally we might come across an opera-loving
esterner like the trail-boss Reece (Glenn Ford) in Delmer
ves' *Cowboy* (1958), who looks with amused contempt on
y-dwellers who do not share his passion: 'You live in
icago, you call yourself civilised and you don't know about
opera season?' The purpose of *Cowboy* was iconoclastic –
take the known conventions of the genre and the articles of

127

the cowboy code and turn them on their heads in the name
realism.*

Lately we have been regaled with a couple of tired lawm
in *Pistolero of Red River* (1967) and *Death of a Gunfigh*
(1969), who escape from their offices and the towns tl
despise for a little quiet fishing. Home-made entertainments
the form of singing and informal parties are a feature
numerous pictures, rarely more touchingly presented than
4th of July gathering in *Shane*, and never more eloquently than
the dance on the foundations of the half-built Tombstone chur
in *My Darling Clementine*, though comparable instances abou
in Ford's work. Nevertheless, the overwhelming impress
Westerns give, and it is by no means a misleading one, is that
leisure time of cowboys was devoted to drinking, whori
fighting and playing poker. The inevitable main street saloon
varying degrees of opulence, is generally the focus for all th
activities, frequently simultaneously. All of them are essentia
male pursuits, and the only one which does not more or l
correspond to some specific physical need is poker.

Now poker, to those who are not obsessed by it, is a ratl
tedious business which in the scale of card games stands
terms of simplicity and chance near the bottom rung – so
way above Faro but a long way below the top marked
Bridge. Like the other Western game, Blackjack, it is a cont
of individuals and, in the many forms now popular,
indigenous American game. Yet despite the simple rules
would guess that a minority of moviegoers understand how
play it. Consequently poker must be seen as in some w

---

* It is ironic, though by no means inappropriate, that as the source
Cowboy, a film which sought to tell the unvarnished truth about West
life, director Daves should have gone to *My Reminiscences as a Cowboy*
account of his few months on a cattle drive by the literary adventurer Fr
Harris, the most notorious liar of his time. When asked if he'd ever kn
Harris to tell the truth, Max Beerbohm replied: 'Sometimes, don't you k
– when his invention flagged.'

ntral to the Western mystique – for surely an intrinsic inter-
t in the game cannot have sustained it over the years as such
a important part of the genre.

Poker in the Western is at once a deeply serious activity and
marginal one. Success is defined more by character than by
kill, and personalities are determined by their attitude to the
ame and the way they play it. Those who devote themselves
olely to poker as professionals, whether they be winners or
osers, can never be accorded the centre of the stage, though
iey may have a certain superficial attraction for the audience
ad for women within the film.

Harking back to my Kennedy–Goldwater thesis, it is inter-
sting to note that John F. Kennedy was a naval war hero
Goldwater too has a distinguished record in the air force),
hile Richard Nixon, also a naval officer in the Pacific, appar-
atly spent much of his off-duty time with a supply unit playing
oker – a fitting occupation for a fashionable anti-hero of the
osurdist *Catch 22 – M*A*S*H* school. (As suggested earlier,
iere does seem to be a place for the Nixon Western.)

Returning to myth and the Western (and almost reversing
oles), in the various films about the Wyatt Earp–Doc Holliday
elationship Holliday is usually the more colourful figure, but
is role is invariably secondary to the dour marshal. The hero
n the other hand must be capable of acquitting himself well at
ae gambling table as proof of his manhood. Yet he should view
ae game philosophically and with detachment, as does Henry
'onda's Earp in *My Darling Clementine*. 'Sir, I really like
oker – every hand has its different problems,' he says, while
stablishing his necessary ability to spot and outwit a cheat.
Iaturally no one can ever hope to base his career on an ability
o cheat, and the cardsharp is inexorably bound to finish up
ead. A deliberately ironic exception to this is the open,
nchallenged cheating by the octoroon gunslinger (Yul
Brynner) in *Invitation to a Gunfighter* (1964), where his object
s not profit but to expose the pusillanimity of the townspeople

who have hired him to carry out their dirty work. The gener
public acceptance of this convention and the ethic it proposes
only too obviously the inspiration which led three directo
almost simultaneously to make their eponymous heroes profe
sional gamblers: Frank Perry's *Doc* (1971), looking at 188
Tombstone from the tubercular dentist's point of view; Robe
Altman's *McCabe and Mrs Miller* (1971); and John Huston
The Life and Times of Judge Roy Bean (1972), in which th
commentary tells us that poker played as great a part in th
winning of the West as the Colt revolver or the covered wago
– a contention not so much true or false as meaningless.

There is perhaps an analogy between poker and the Wester
movie: one could say that it forms a microcosm or more accu
ately a paradigm of the form. In addition to the aspects alread
mentioned, the game might be seen as a steady progression, i
which courses of action are undisclosed, towards a final confront
tion between two men, the more circumspect and fainthearte
(usually identified as the married, the marginally secure and th
weak) having dropped out on the way and thrown in their han
Even when not playing poker, Westerners (and now peopl
generally) resort to its terminology: the showdown, the fou
flusher, calling someone's bluff, keeping a poker face.

Andrew Sarris has made out a case for regarding the Bud
Boetticher–Randolph Scott Westerns as metaphorical poke
games, though to the best of my recollection no actual game
are ever played in them. They are, he says, 'constructed partl
as allegorical odysseys and partly as floating poker game
where every character takes turns at bluffing about his han
until the final showdown.'*

There is, however, so far as I know, only one horse opera
the 'chamber Western' *A Big Hand for the Little Lady* (196€
British title: *Big Deal at Dodge City*), devoted exclusively t
poker. In it a pioneering husband-and-wife cardsharping tea

---

* *The American Cinema* (E. P. Dutton, New York, 1964), p. 124.

oker school in *A Big Hand for the Little Lady*

hakes down a poker school made up of prosperous and gull-
ble leading citizens of Laredo. The wife, affecting ignorance of
he game, takes over the poor hand of her 'ailing' husband to
aise the ante and deliver the *coup de grâce*. A lot depends upon
he con-man husband being played by Henry Fonda, whose
presence serves to disarm both audience and fellow players
before the gimmick ending, which would no doubt have been
more effective in the short television play from which the over-
extended movie was derived. Another equally tedious Western,
5 *Card Stud* (1968), the poorest exercise in the genre by the
usually reliable Henry Hathaway, turns upon a single poker
game. Here a mad preacher (Robert Mitchum), who carries his
gun in a Bible, kills off one by one the other players in a game
which had resulted in the lynching of his cardsharp brother. A
highly obtrusive device in the film is the repetition of overhead
shots re-creating the position of the participants in the game.

Pursuing his debatable contention that the Western hero is

Five aces (*The Deadly Companions*); and (*right*) jack of diamonds and ace of hearts (*One Eyed Jacks*)

pre-eminently a man of leisure, Robert Warshow saw poker as 'a game which perfectly expresses his talent for remaining relaxed in the midst of tension.' His point is well taken if one emphasises that incipient violence is always present in that tension, that a false move or accusation can bring it on. It is not without good reason that in that most calculated of recent entertainments, *Butch Cassidy and the Sundance Kid*, when we first see the eponymous heroes together they are forcing a gambler to back down. In fact, after the sweaty, heavy breathing, laconic challenges, shot in an elegantly lit sepia-tone, all that is eventually needed to make the vexatious challenge withdraw is to hear his opponent's name. The ethical basis for this conflict is by no means clear; whereas in *Invitation to a Gunfighter* a man of probity deliberately cheats, the Sundance Kid is a figure of dubious credentials merely claiming that he has played a straight game. Perhaps one is splitting hairs, but

132

proud hired gun in the former seems to be engaged in a
serious moral challenge, while Butch Cassidy and his sidekick
are merely asserting the superiority of their style.

The moral judgment proposed by the code of poker provides
the central motif for Brando's *One Eyed Jacks*, and the striking
opening image of Peckinpah's *The Deadly Companions*, both of
which draw on the traditional symbolic power and visual
beauty of playing cards – qualities seized on outside the
Western in gambling pictures like the marathon poker movie
The Cincinatti Kid (1965), which began as a Peckinpah
project, though he was subsequently fired, and the fortune-
telling scene shot in colour as a prelude to Agnès Varda's
otherwise black-and-white picture *Cléo de Cinq à Sept* (1961).
In Brando's film, a distant reworking of the Pat Garrett–Billy
the Kid story, his central characters are one-eyed Jacks. The
treacherous hypocrite Dad Longworth (Karl Malden), the
essentially evil man, shows a good face to society; Rio
(Brando), the misunderstood outlaw, shows a bad one. Their
real faces are the concealed ones.*

Again, in the opening of *The Deadly Companions*, we are
confronted with a close-up of a body suspended from the
ceiling with its feet on a barrel and five aces pinned to the
shirt. We thus have imposed upon us an overwhelming judgment on the man before we even see his sly features and
register the mysterious, equivocal relationship between him
and the withdrawn, poker-faced man who cuts him down.

Setting aside the internal moral significance of poker, there

* In gambling argot the movie's title refers to the only one-eyed Jack in
the pack – the Jack of Diamonds – and the film clearly implies a symbiotic
relationship between the film's two knaves of a kind I have mentioned
earlier. Card-playing experts, I believe, have noted other possible elements
in the film's symbolism, both in relation to poker and to the variations of the
game 'Seven Up', and so have students of the more arcane aspects of playing
card iconography. Critics interested in the sexual symbolism of the genre
have suggested that the title slyly invokes a slang expression for the penis.

is a further use to which the game has been put as a criticism of a way of life. In Penn's *Little Big Man,* Wild Bill Hickok is ignominiously shot down at a poker table and dies unheroically, his neck bizarrely cradled by the boot of a fellow gambler. In *The Stalking Moon*, a halfbreed scout, who acts as the film's chorus and commentator, suggests with cheerful irony that he should teach the rules of poker to anyone seeking to be assimilated into white 'civilisation': 'You gonna be white – you better learn the white man's game,' he tells the uncomprehending halfbreed boy at the centre of the film's metaphysical tug-of-war.

Far more emphatic than either of these is the insertion into the middle of John Ford's last Western, *Cheyenne Autumn*, of a Dodge City interlude which worried many critics and puzzled audiences so much that it was wholly or partially removed from some copies of the film. This sequence is shot in an entirely different style from the sombre, near-tragic mood which informs the rest of the film. Here we see a lazy, cynical, unscrupulous Wyatt Earp (James Stewart) and Doc Holliday (Arthur Kennedy), as different from their counterparts in *My Darling Clementine* as the treatment of the Cheyenne is from Ford's approach to Indians in his earlier films. Opulently dressed and sitting in the Dodge City saloon-cum-whorehouse from which they so obviously derive their good fortune, they drink and play poker totally unmoved by the suffering and depravity around them. The tone of this scene is farcical and indulgent, reeking of corruption, self-interest and indifference. By the indirection of caricature, irony and artifice Ford came eventually to a possibly more authentic depiction of Holliday and Earp than he did through the apparently 'realistic' surface of *My Darling Clementine*. From the gambling tables of Dodge City, by way of a burlesque chase of a single, starving Indian accidentally strayed into the vicinity which came to be known as 'The Battle of Dodge City', we return to the Cheyenne continuing their bitter journey from a desolate exile back to the tribe's confiscated hunting grounds.

The history of the American West has been the story of the accelerating intrusion of civilisation into virgin territory. There came first the trapper and fur trader and the disinterested explorer travelling on foot or by canoe. Then the transient miner (usually a dubious character in Westerns), the rancher and the farmer on horseback and with wagon trains, accompanied by the establishment of military bases. Primitive forms of communication like the stagecoach and the pony express are gradually supplemented, then replaced, by the train and the telegraph. With a suitable degree of nostalgia each of these phases has been dealt with in the Western, and we must remember that the elegiac strain in a notably bitter and reactionary form is to be found as early as Fenimore Cooper, writing in the 1830s, which is to say well before the period of Western development that the cowboy movie treats. The wonders of nineteenth-century technology, the idea of inevitable and beneficial progress, have been celebrated in movies dedicated to singing the praises of *The Iron Horse* (1924), *Union Pacific* (1939), *Western Union* (1941), and the engineering feats attendant upon linking America coast-to-coast.

As the locomotive has declined in significance, its already considerable appeal has increased: the steam train is kept alive today partly by a few devoted railway buffs but mainly by the movie industry. One might look upon it as the great creator of

'The ugly intrusion of the modern world': the end of *The Ballad of Cable Hogue* (Stella Stevens, Jason Robards)

community, as opposed to the car which is a private vehicle disruptive of community feeling. Only in the last fifteen years has the horseless carriage seriously entered the Western, and it has done so not as a harbinger of the brave new world but as a symbol of a deadening mass society and a dehumanised technology.

I put it this way because its deployment is something more than a simple-minded Luddism; it reflects in fact not an attitude contemporary to the turn of the century, but current feelings about the shortcomings and blindnesses of our over-mechanised, polluted, unbalanced, disintegrating environment. Just take the progressively lethal use of the car by Sam Peckinpah. *Guns in the Afternoon* (1962) opens with an old marshal nearly being knocked down by a horseless carriage, possibly the first he has seen; in *The Wild Bunch*, the degenerate Mexican local dictator Mapache (a man, like post-World War II American technology, under the tutelage of German

he unromantic view: *Will Penny* (Charlton Heston)

xperts) is fascinated both by his new machine-gun and his little
d Tin Lizzie, and eventually uses the latter to drag the
lexican member of the bunch around town in the dust; in *The
allad of Cable Hogue*, the eponymous hero, whose stagecoach
atering post will shortly be made redundant by the internal
mbustion engine, is killed when the brake slips on the first
ar he has ever touched.

A major preoccupation of the Western in the Sixties and
eventies has been the ugly intrusion of the modern world – the
onymous, rationalising conglomerate corporations which in
onte Walsh run the ranches from Wall Street and bring
nemployment to the cowboys; the civil servants and bureau-
ats in *McClintock!*; the politicians in *The Man Who Shot
iberty Valance*; the businessmen and civic boosters in *Death
a Gunfighter* and *The Good Guys and the Bad Guys*. There
, however, a gulf in fact and myth between the Western and

137

modern society which the cinema cannot bridge. A movie like Anthony Mann's last and only disappointing Western *Cimarron* (1960), based on Edna Ferber's epic novel, attempts the task with uneven results, by tracing the hero's career up to his death in World War I and showing developments in the community he has helped found after the Oklahoma land rush of 1889, but has deserted for other last frontiers, gold rushes and the Cuban War. The picture has a great void at its centre.

Even more so has *How the West Was Won* (1962), the first feature film using the Cinerama process, which spends three hours synopsising every known Western situation in the tale of three generations of a pioneer family between 1840 and 1890 before making a breathtaking jump to present-day America. At one moment the screen is showing a retired sheriff and his family heading towards a new home in an untrammelled landscape after the last bandit has been shot down; the next moment we are regaled with a vertiginous montage of aerial shots of car-choked Los Angeles freeways and flyovers, and so forth. There is no suggestion elsewhere in the movie that its producers are doing anything but celebrating America, and in consequence we are expected to accept this coda as the marvellous visionary future which the pioneers struggled for and which has now been realised by their proud successors. A black humorist could scarcely have come up with a bleaker, more satirical ending.

Jumping with the makers of *How the West Was Won* from the winning of the West to the problems of coping with the present, we come to a group of movies I have referred to earlier as Modern or Post-Westerns. These are films about the West today, and draw upon the Western itself or more generally on 'the cowboy cult'.

A few movies, like Burt Kennedy's engaging *The Rounders* (1965) and Stuart Rosenberg's aimless *Pocket Money* (1972) deal in a fairly realistic manner with the hardships of working on the range today, in similar fashion to the way such movies as

138

owboy and *Will Penny* present an unromantic view of the nineteenth-century cowpuncher's life. Quite a number of films look at the less glamorous underside of the cowboy's role as professional rodeo entertainer, where his traditional skills are divorced from day-to-day utility and placed at the service of a public spectacle nearly as dangerous as bull-fighting. In the early Fifties there were several films of this type – most notably Nicholas Ray's *The Lusty Men* (1952), but also Boetticher's low budget *Bronco Buster* (1952). Recently there has been a crop of such films – Cliff Robertson's *J. W. Coop*, the late Steve Ihnat's *The Honkers*, and Sam Peckinpah's *Junior Bonner*, all released in 1972 and taking an equally disenchanted view of present-day America.

Seen out of his time and place, the Western hero seems an incongruous figure. Depending on the dramatic use to which he may be put, he can be variously seen as vulnerable and pathetic or dangerous and anarchic, an upholder of cherished traditional values or the embodiment of outmoded ways which linger menacingly on, a challenge to modern conformity or the incarnation of a past that must be rejected. There are many examples of this outside the Western. In American fiction there Earle Shoop in Nathanael West's *The Day of the Locust*, Joe Buck in James Leo Herlihy's *Midnight Cowboy*, Buck Loner in Gore Vidal's *Myra Breckinridge*, the last two of which have been filmed. In scripting Carol Reed's *The Third Man* (1949), Graham Greene cast around for the most fitting occupation for Holly Martins, the naive American thrown among the cynical sophisticates of corrupt postwar Vienna, and decided to make him an author of pulp Western fiction who had never set foot in the West; the only person who genuinely befriends Martins is a English NCO who has read his novels. (One wonders if Greene had seen Jean Renoir's 1935 film *Le Crime de Monsieur Lange*, in which the eponymous hero, a sad though resilient employee of a shoddy Parisian publishing house, realises his dreams through stories about his imaginary

Western hero 'Arizona Jim', the popular success of whose adventures are seized upon by his unscrupulous boss and become the centre of the film's dramatic and moral structure. Then there are the contrasting performances by Andy Griffith in two movies of the Fifties: the illiterate backwoods buffoon disrupting airforce life in the comedy *No Time for Sergeants* (1958), and the guitar-twanging demagogue who threatens America with a home-grown totalitarianism in Elia Kazan's overwrought *A Face in the Crowd* (1956). Perhaps most striking of all is Major King Kong (played by Slim Pickens in one of his rare non-Western appearances), the Texan pilot in *Dr Strangelove* who puts on his stetson when the red alert comes and rides the hydrogen bomb which will destroy the world as if it were a bucking bronco in a rodeo show.

In marked contrast to these figures is Sam the Lion (Ben Johnson), the retired rancher who keeps the conscience of the decaying Texas township in Peter Bogdanovich's *The Last Picture Show* (1971). And oddly enough, in Antonioni's curiously callow and unfeeling *Zabriskie Point* (1970), the only genuinely affecting image is in his single reference to the cowboy cult. This occurs in the desert café after his tiresome heroine has departed. Sitting at the bar is a leathery old cowboy, impassive, silent and perfectly still. He has been quite indifferent to the girl's presence, and now the camera lingers on him, viewing him through a window and giving the impression that what we are seeing is a combination of a portrait by Andrew Wyeth or Edward Hopper and a sentimental Norman Rockwell cover for *Saturday Evening Post*.

The most striking Post-Westerns are John Sturges' *Bad Day at Black Rock* (1954), John Huston's *The Misfits* (1960), David Miller's *Lonely are the Brave* (1962), Martin Ritt's *Hud* (1963) and Don Siegel's *Coogan's Bluff* (1968). Central to them all is the way in which the characters are influenced by, or are victims of, the cowboy cult; they intensify and play on the audience's feelings about, and knowledge of, Western movies.

140

Bad Day at Black Rock has something resembling a
estern plot. A one-armed stranger (Spencer Tracy) gets off
e train one morning in a small Nevada town to be greeted
ith suspicion and hostility, which turns into a series of at-
mpts to scare him away and then kill him when it transpires
at he is seeking to meet a local Japanese farmer called
omoko. The year is 1945, just after the end of the war, and
e stranger is an ex-army officer who wants to give the farmer
e posthumously awarded medal his son had won in Italy
nile saving Tracy's life. The intruder is at first fobbed off with
e story that Komoko had been interned along with other
isei after Pearl Harbor; he later discovers that the man has
en murdered after a patriotic drunken orgy marking the
ming of the war, and that moreover he had already built up
cal resentment by finding water on a tract of apparently
orthless land sold him by the local boss (Robert Ryan).
Black Rock works admirably as a thriller and was among
e most interesting of early CinemaScope movies in its use of
lised groupings and elaborate dramatic compositions.*
hat is also of interest is that the film could never have been
ade at the time it was set in and was, I think, the first to touch
on the still highly controversial matter of the deplorable

---

* The cameraman was the late William C. Mellor, a frequent collaborator
George Stevens; he also shot the most elaborately composed of all
thony Mann Westerns, *The Last Frontier*. The role of the cameraman
of paramount importance in the cowboy movie, indeed in the cinema
nerally, and I regret my incompetence to handle the subject adequately.
e contributions to the Western of Lucien Ballard (most of Peckinpah,
veral Boetticher films, *Will Penny*, *The Raid*, *The Proud Ones*, etc.),
oyd Crosby (*High Noon*, *The Wonderful Country*), Charles B. Lang (*The
an From Laramie*, *The Magnificent Seven*, *One Eyed Jacks*), James Wong
owe (*Hud* and *Hombre*), William Clothier (who has worked with
etticher, Ford, Peckinpah, McLaglen, Wayne, Walsh and Burt Kennedy,
well as servicing exciting surprises from unknown talents like *Dragoon
ells Massacre* and *Firecreek*), and a dozen other cameramen, cannot be
errated – yet cannot be fully measured.

treatment Japanese Americans were subjected to during Worl War II. The producer was Dore Schary, who ten years befor had sought to use the Western genre for his wartime propaganda picture *Storm in the West*.

But what really concerns me here is the picture's attitude the West. Despite an apparent absence of cattle, the Westerner are very insistent upon their status as cowboys. For exampl the desk clerk at the unoccupied local hotel tells Tracy in a fl monotone that the hotel is 'reserved for cowboys, for the every wish and comfort' when they are in town. When Trac gets a room he is ousted from it by the lethargically menacin Lee Marvin, who stretches out on the bed and tells him: 'The rooms are reserved for cowboys, for their every wish an comfort when they are in town, and I'm in town as any fool ca see.' The snarling xenophobe Ryan tells Tracy, 'We' suspicious of strangers here – a hangover from the Old West to which Tracy replies, 'I thought the tradition of the Old We was hospitality.' And Ryan goes on to make a vicious litt speech about the general public and their 'Wild West', the businessmen and their 'undeveloped West', the writers an their 'romantic West' – 'To us this place is *our* West and I wis they'd leave us alone.'

The clear purpose of the film is to locate in the all-America figure of the cowboy some less attractive native trait patriotism masking xenophobia, ignorance masquerading intuitive common-sense, mindless aggression concealed beneat virility, arrogance disguised as style. In addition they can even fight fair, although a little skill at karate and a touch intelligence by their one-armed opponent is more than enoug to defeat them.

Hud Bannon (Paul Newman) would be very much at hom in Black Rock, yet there is a genuine attempt in *Hud* to reve this unattractive young Texan as a perversion of Wester ideals, the decadent fag end of a tradition seen at its best in h father (Melvyn Douglas), a fine old rancher who spurns the lu

f oil and sticks to breeding longhorns 'to remind me of the
ay things was – everything we have comes from them.' The
Western guitar music on the soundtrack belongs to the old
an; the debased Country and Western music which issues
om juke-boxes in seedy cafés and the radio in Hud's battered
adillac reflects the ambience of Hud himself. The twentieth
century they both reject overtakes them when their cattle are
fected by foot-and-mouth disease. Hud's response is to try to
vade the law by driving the stock elsewhere, his father's to
ce the consequences – which necessarily involves his death
d the extinction of his world. Together they watch a bull-
ozer cut a pit for the cattle to be driven into, gunned down by
overnment agents in hygienic masks and boots and then
uried in lime. It is a sickening scene which speaks for itself
ithout the old man's sententious gloss (only too typical unfor-
nately of Martin Ritt) that 'It doesn't take long to kill things
ke it does to grow.'

There are two other important figures in *Hud*. One is Alma,
e ranch's housekeeper; in a performance of depth and matur-
y by Patricia Neal, this bruised and intelligent woman stands
r the kind of complex absorption in modern life, that commit-
ent to reality, which Hud and the old man have avoided. The
ther character, through whose eyes the action is mostly seen,
Hud's nephew Lon, who begins by hero-worshipping Hud
d grows to see his desperate shortcomings. Little by little the
untry changes because of the men they admire, his grand-
ther tells him. It is scarcely a coincidence, indeed it is part of
e film's resonance, that Lon is played by the 20-year-old
randon De Wilde, who ten years before appeared as little
ey, the child through whose eyes much of *Shane* is seen.

The Misfits and *Lonely Are the Brave* take a different, more
omantic view of the cowboy, though they put him down in as
nglamorous and rebarbative a world. Leaving aside the import-
t aspect of *The Misfits* which concerns screenwriter Arthur
iller's attempt to explore the personality of his then wife

Marilyn Monroe, the theme of the movie is the degradation and dissolution of the American Dream. And the chosen method is to concentrate on a party of rootless, aimless cowboys living round Reno, Nevada, divorce capital of America and graveyard of romance. The group is composed of the ironically named cowboy Gay (Clark Gable), a punch-drunk, mother-fixated rodeo rider (Montgomery Clift), a pathetic, garrulous aviator (Eli Wallach) who lives in a half-completed house, and a recent divorcée (Monroe) whose exterior *joie de vivre* conceals an emotional numbness. Together they set off into the mountains to hunt wild stallions with a truck and an aeroplane – a quest which is finally abandoned when the girl discovers to her horror that the object of this heroic exercise is to collect horse meat to be processed into tinned cat food. The film ends oddly, mystically, with Gay and the girl driving beneath the stars, having apparently discovered some peace in nothingness. At the time this scene, and the picture generally, seemed portentous and pretentious; over the years, however, *The Misfits* has gained an unusual and affecting depth as a work about the Monroe charisma (it was her last completed film) and the fading charm of Clark Gable, whose last appearance this was.

Jack Burns (Kirk Douglas) in *Lonely Are the Brave* is another misfit, a 'don't fence me in' cowboy almost identical with the barbed-wire-hating Ryan Dempsey played by Douglas in *Man Without a Star* (1955). Only now he is in modern New Mexico, where jet vapour fills the sky, Boot Hill has been replaced by an automobile scrapyard, and motor highways have taken over from dirt trails. Subtlety is not exactly the most obvious quality of the film, and the makers do little to conceal their utter loathing of modern America and all its works. (The screenplay is by Dalton Trumbo, most talented of the 'Hollywood Ten', the first victims of the postwar unAmerican Activities Committee witchhunt.) On the other hand, apart from a sadistic prison guard, most of the other characters are approached sympathetically. The sheriff (Walter

145

(*above*) *The Misfits:* dissolution of the American Dream; (*below*) *Lonely Are t*
Brave: modern cowboy and modern technology

Matthau), who reluctantly heads the posse which pursues Burns when he foolishly breaks from jail, hopes that he will get away with his attempt to escape across the mountains. This lawman is disgusted with his lifeless, characterless police force as well as with the local army base, whose commanding officer sees the hunt as good practice for his helicopter pilots. The film is an early example of the use so often made since of the helicopter as a menacing symbol of totalitarianism and anonymous technology, and the sheriff anticipates the attitude of the reluctant leader of the posse (Robert Ryan) in *The Wild Bunch*, who says of the trash accompanying him: 'We're after men and I wish to God I was with them.'

Lonely Are the Brave could also be said to anticipate the climax of Peckinpah's *Cable Hogue*, for the film's structure is founded on the inexorable collision of Burns and his horse and a truck carrying a load of lavatory pans. We are introduced to this van when its indigestion-ridden driver stops in Joplin, Missouri, and announces he is heading for Duke City, New Mexico; and from then on the film constantly cuts back to this inelegant, impersonal juggernaut beneath the wheels of which the doomed Burns will be sacrificed as he tries to ride across a rain-slick road to the Mexican border. All that remains after the dying cowboy has been driven off in an ambulance is his stetson, lying in a puddle illuminated by the lights of passing cars.

In all the attention devoted to the hopeless rebellion of Burns, it is possible to overlook the rather unimpressive presence of his friend – a left-wing writer serving two years in jail for helping illegal Mexican immigrants. Offered as a practical rebel in contrast to the romantic intransigence of Burns, he has now decided to quit the wild life they both enjoyed and devote himself to working for social reform within the system. In the era of Kennedy and Martin Luther King, this seemed an obvious and desirable alternative; it still does, but it is a difficult thing to dramatise, and such a man has not been easy to accommodate in the Western, nor has he appealed much to

147

Coogan's Bluff: the Arizona lawman (Clint Eastwood) surveys Manhattan

those creating the prevailing fashions in the radical, liberated Hollywood of the past ten years.

Unlike the other four Modern Westerns I have discussed, *Coogan's Bluff* is largely set in urban America after an opening sequence which locates the brutal, confident deputy sheriff Coogan (Clint Eastwood) in his natural habitat of rural Arizona. There we see him in a jeep tracking down a wife-murderer who has fled from a Navajo reservation and gone native. Cheerfully dispensing with the niceties of legal procedure which hamper his urban colleagues, he calls upon his pathetic victim to 'Put your hands up, Chief', and then knocks him down with a gun-butt.

Coogan's next assignment is to go to New York and bring back a fugitive prisoner, a drug-taking psychopathic hippie, and the events of this opening sequence are paralleled by the less happy, less successful progress around Manhattan, where he becomes embroiled in a world more complicated than his simple Western life and finds himself meeting a contempt similar to that he had shown his Indian prisoner. A Negro plainclothes-man refers to him as 'Buffalo Bill with the fancy hat'; a witness he tries to railroad informs him that 'This isn't the O.K. Corral around here'; everybody calls him 'Texas', and a whore he rejects snarls 'Texas faggot'.

His principal critic is the hard-pressed New York precinct cop, Lt McElroy (Lee J. Cobb), who looks at Coogan as if he's a primitive man from another time and place. 'What gives with you people out there – too much sun?' he asks, and when the injured Coogan tries to explain why he has to go after the prisoner whom he has foolishly allowed to escape, McElroy shrugs his shoulders with sardonic resignation and says, 'I know, a man's gotta do what a man's gotta do.'

The humour and criticism is not all directed at Coogan's gaucherie and the limitations of his crude, simple values. His genuine style is a challenge to the role-playing manner of so many New Yorkers he runs into; through his eyes we see the nastiness and run-down state of Manhattan. Some of this feeling is summed up in a close-up of his polished, pointed boot stepping out of a taxi into a pile of garbage in the street. And despite the patronising air with which he is greeted, his clothes and bearing have a powerful, in some cases almost fetishist, appeal for many people he meets. Moreover Coogan may have simple-minded and dangerous notions about life, but he isn't a naïve buffoon after the fashion of numerous cowboys in sophisticated urban comedies or *Midnight Cowboy's* Joe Buck. The audience may be happy to see this arrogant Westerner disconcerted and humiliated, but we are also touched by his frustration and bewilderment.

Unfortunately *Coogan's Bluff* loses this critical balance about halfway through, and from being an intelligent, ironic movie it plunges into a crude thriller which intentionally or not appears to be a vindication of Coogan's aggression and crude 'law 'n' order' tactics. Indeed quite a different mood

149

overtakes the later part of the film. Apart from a certain vague humanity (Coogan at the end gives his prisoner a cigarette whereas he has refused one to his Indian prisoner at the beginning), the Arizonan appears to have learned nothing, and the New York cop seems only to have learned where Coogan comes from: 'Give my regards to Tex – I mean Arizona,' is his parting shot in a rather sentimental closing scene. In fact, after the illegal procedures he has resorted to, Coogan would never have been able to leave New York with his prisoner, and that would have been a more interesting and logical ending. It was no doubt with this in mind that three years later Eastwood and his director Don Siegel made another police thriller, and in *Dirty Harry* the action turns precisely upon a dangerous criminal being set free as a result of the illegal means employed in making the arrest.

Between these two films Siegel had directed Eastwood in the stolid Mexican Western *Two Mules for Sister Sara* and the subdued little Civil War Grand Guignol piece *The Beguiled*. On the side, Siegel had taken over and completed (without credit) the unsatisfactory but underrated Richard Widmark 'changing times' Western *Death of a Gunfighter*, and advised Eastwood on his directorial debut, *Play Misty for Me*. While I regard *Dirty Harry* as a powerful fable and a dazzling display of filmcraft, I cannot say that I am entirely happy about the political and social implications of the film. Yet in making it, Siegel and Eastwood faced head on the problems posed by *Coogan's Bluff* – they could not possibly have resorted to the Western for their solution without implying an observation of legal niceties wholly inappropriate to the genre and frontier life.

Like the makers of Westerns, the genre's critics tend to locate their ideal in the past. George Fenin and William Everson, authors of the only major American book on the subject, *The Western from Silent to Cinerama*, would place the Golden Age around 1920, when their beloved William S. Hart was at his eak. For them the best Westerns of the Fifties are Henry athaway's admirable *From Hell to Texas*, because of a script ecalling at times the simplicity of William S. Hart', and *hane*, 'which sent one's mind scurrying back to William art's *The Toll Gate*.' Both Robert Warshow and Harry chein in their 1954 essays strongly implied that the genre was pproaching its final sunset, and a dozen years later, in his 966 radio talk *Decline of the Western*, Laurence Kitchen oiced a fairly general feeling that the great days were over, ough just where the line should be drawn he left vague. All at weekly movie critics need is a succession of lousy cowboy lms followed by an impressive 'anti-Western' like *Hud* or *Ionte Walsh* to turn their ready-made sermon on the subject to a reading of the last rites over the genre's sinking coffin. I ention this in no spirit of reproach, for the response is easily nderstandable.

This approach, however, flies in the face of the facts – by hich I mean of course that it runs counter to my own opinion. s I have suggested earlier, the Western seems to me far from oribund – indeed I should go so far as to regard it as one of e more vital centres of the cinema and the popular arts in our me. Admittedly, I think it is unlikely that we shall ever again e a director of John Ford's stature channel so much of his ergy into the genre. From *Stagecoach* in 1939 to *Cheyenne utumn* in 1964, he towered over the Western, and for some me to come his presence will continue to be felt. In Ford's adow, the Fifties were dominated by Anthony Mann, Delmer aves, Budd Boetticher and John Sturges, and the Sixties by am Peckinpah. And to each decade Howard Hawks con- ibuted a single movie, part of an evolving personal cycle with hn Wayne always at the centre: *Red River* (1948), *Rio Bravo* 959), *El Dorado* (1967) and finally *Rio Lobo* (1970). The ots and situations of the last three are almost identical – a air of increasingly elderly lawmen accompanied by valetudin- rian eccentrics and laconic, sympathetic youngsters upholding

e law in the face of venal, faceless opponents. One has to view
e films a second time and in the right order to appreciate that
ie isn't seeing a series of fading carbon copies where the
omedy gets broader as the dramatic grip slackens, but rather a
radual digging deeper into familiar themes, where the looser
irface conceals a profound pessimism, as if the ageing of
awks and his heroes were being equated with the ageing, the
ss of energy, of America itself.

There is now, I fancy, no need for any director to devote
mself to the Western. It is easier today to avoid getting typed,
sier to raise money for personal movies which fit no par-
cular genre. When a young unknown like Dick Richards
akes *The Culpepper Cattle Company*, or an experienced
oducer like Stuart Millar elects to make his directorial debut
ith *When the Legends Die*, or Robert Altman comes up with
cCabe and Mrs Miller, we know that they have deliberately
iosen to make a Western, that what they wished to say was
culiarly suited to that form and setting. And we do not
cessarily expect them to return to the genre immediately, or
all. Of all major directors today, only Sam Peckinpah is
tally identified with Westerns, and on the two occasions when
has deserted the genre the results have been disappointing
he Getaway, 1972) or disastrous (*Straw Dogs*, 1971): in
ch case the pictures failed to create a convincing world from
e trappings of the chosen contemporary milieu (respectively,
xas and Cornwall), and both could have been easily, happily
insposed to the West. Two other directors continue to
ecialise in Westerns at a much lower, yet not negligible, level
Andrew McLaglen, a protégé of John Ford, whose assistant
was on several occasions, and Burt Kennedy, screenwriter
r Boetticher. They are hit-and-miss artists, notable more for
imina than for consistent vision or imagination, though
ither is to be despised. Acolytes both, they loyally tend the
me at their mentor's altar and seem unlikely to become high
iests themselves.

153

pair of increasingly elderly lawmen': Robert Mitchum and John Wayne, with
thur Hunnicutt, in Howard Hawks' *El Dorado*

Meanwhile the genre flourishes, some movies contributing to its vitality, others merely attesting to its cultural centrality. As in the past, almost as many films sink their vampire fangs in its body as provide it with a transfusion of new blood. George Englund's embarrassing hard-rock musical *Zachariah* (1970) for instance, is a biblical allegory that announced itself as the first 'electric Western' and featured a number of pop groups in subsidiary roles. Another biblical Western is Robert Downey's immoderately ambitious *Greaser's Palace* (1972), a random anachronistic satire in which a zoot-suited Christ descends on nineteenth-century New Mexico explaining his mission with the words: 'I'm on my way to Jerusalem to be an actor-singer.' The Holy Ghost appears as a Lone Ranger figure in white shirt and black stetson, and God as a taciturn, bearded old-timer. Christ moves among corrupt saloon owners, permanently drugged Indians, homosexual Mexican dwarfs, restores crippled pioneers, walks on the water, dances in a bar-room (the Mary Magdalene figure complains that 'a man with hole in his hand gets more applause than me'), before being crucified. *Greaser's Palace* (the title, a pun on the grandiose 'Caesar's Palace', suggests Las Vegas as the New Jerusalem) confirms the real difficulties of making a satirical Western. The genre is riding a knife-edge all the time, and Downey's parodies of *High Noon* and Peckinpah are crude to a degree. Basically it's the kind of thing that gives bad taste a bad name.

As a director who has ascended from the underground movie into the world of feature films, Downey provides a link between the pretentious, biblical, showbiz conjunction of *Zachariah* and the flip, lackadaisical, camp farrago *Lonesome Cowboys* (1968), in which the stock company of the Andy Warhol factory go West to Arizona under the direction of Paul Morrissey. This ludicrous movie is a vague transposition of *Romeo and Juliet*. The film occasionally suggests an exploitation of the latent homosexuality in cowboy movies, but generally settles for predictable gay banter and aggressive

154

smuch as the movie has a highlight, it resides in the scene
ere a former ballet dancer demonstrates — using a hitching
l as a dancer's exercise bar — how a cowboy should move
d draw a gun.

Regrettably, Jean-Luc Godard's *Wind From the East* (1970)
ongs right in there with *Zachariah*, *Greaser's Palace* and
nesome Cowboys. According to James Roy MacBean in his
roduction to the published screenplay of *Vent d'Est*, Godard
stematically takes apart the traditional elements of bourgeois
ema — especially as exemplified by the Western — revealing
sometimes hidden, sometimes blatant repressiveness which
derlies it.'* The film is apparently set where the heroine's
cle 'managed the exploitation of aluminium for the Alcoa
mpany near Dodge City' and features a sadistic cavalryman
l a hapless Indian. It is nothing if not an elaborate political
gory or meditation inspired by the Western. But it is a
esome, hectoring film, alternating between the crude and the
scure, and painfully sad in coming from a director who has
itten so personally and sensitively about Ford, Mann and
ckinpah.

Discussing *Wind from the East*, one is reminded of a com-
nt Godard made about Peckinpah in a 1962 interview.
nerican directors, he said, 'have a gift for the kind of sim-
city which brings depth — in a little Western like *Ride the
gh Country*, for instance. If one tries to do something like
t in France, one looks like an intellectual.' One cannot
nestly say that by moving in the opposite direction Godard
nages to be less of an intellectual than he has previously
n, or shows any greater likelihood of contacting the large,
pular audience which has always eluded him. A sojourn in
nerica directing the kind of films he once admired but now
ofesses to despise might well have benefited him and made it
ssible for him to operate within the central tradition of the

---

Lorrimer, London, 1972.

155

cinema rather than on its uninviting, often justly ignore
edges.

Admittedly my politics are of a less extreme and ideologic
kind than Godard's, but having spent much of the first half
1972, between teaching at the University of Texas, travellir
round the West, I don't find it impossible to combine my likir
of Westerns with my love for the 'Real West', my knowledge
frontier history and an awareness of the contemporary world
find little difficulty in reconciling Horace Gregory's attack c
the commercial and political exploitation of the 'cowboy cu
with Harry Schein's defence of the Western movie. In his ess:
Guns of the Roaring West, Gregory wrote:

More than anything else the cult expresses the desire to dramatise
brightly surfaced and thin layer of American history, one that can
read at a glance with the mind untroubled by the need of serio
understanding or research. It is a pictorial short-cut back to feeli
very much at home in the United States.

Where Gregory's *Partisan Review* team-mate Robert Warshc
calls the Western 'an art form for connoisseurs' in that it allo
the spectator to appreciate subtle changes and variations
familiar routines, rituals and patterns, Schein saw the genre
offering far more than aesthetic attractions:

It gives us in fact the opportunity – unique in our culture and histc
– to experience how folklore is made, how it grows and takes sha
The roots of the mythology of Europe and the Near East are hidd
in the past and can be only partially reconstructed today. But Wh
America is no older than Gutenberg. It achieved economic a
consequently cultural independence (an essential prerequisite for
mythology of its own) about the same time as the novel made
artistic breakthrough and started reaching a public. It is no
incidence that James Fenimore Cooper is America's first origi
contributor to literature. It is just as natural that the cinema e
braced the Western from the start. In less than a lifetime of c
generation it has developed from something seemingly insignific

a tightly designed mythology following its own laws, to become young America's own folklore.

e dialectical relationship between the opposing contentions Gregory and Schein is neither purely aesthetic nor mythical; the same time it cannot be regarded as a simple conflict tween art and honestly recorded history. 'Humankind cannot ar very much reality,' observed T. S. Eliot (a poet born in St uis, the point at which the West begins); nor can the estern. The genre can tolerate, indeed invites, transfusions of ality in the form of convincing psychological relationships d persuasively shoddy decor − every decade has its own ndards in the matter of realism. Ford's *My Darling ementine* looked pretty realistic by the prevailing standards 1946, though it was at every point a total misrepresentation the events leading up to the gunfight at the O.K. Corral, even year of which it gets wrong. The subsequent versions of the me story move ever nearer to the known facts − John urges' *The Gunfight at the O.K. Corral* (1957), the same ector's *Hour of the Gun* (1967), and Frank Perry's *Doc* 971) − and each in turn presents a grubbier, more disen-anted view of life in Tombstone. But no version arrives at that ality of truth, albeit a bogus, mythic one, which Ford achieves. The sordid real life story of Wyatt Earp and Doc Holliday is gely of interest to us now for the light it throws on the way ir legendary reputations have been shaped rather than for y intrinsic importance they had. The same is true of Billy nney and Jesse James, and in Arthur Penn's Billy the Kid m, *The Left-Handed Gun* (1958), and Nicholas Ray's *The ue Story of Jesse James* (1956), the central characters are amined in terms of, and personally confronted with, the yths which they became in their own lifetimes. In *The Man ho Shot Liberty Valance* (1961), which comes closer than y of his other Westerns to a destruction of the myth, Ford esents two stories − the long-accepted one by which Senator

157

Versions of history: *The Gunfight at the O.K. Corral, Hour of the Gun* an
(*opposite*) *Doc*

Stoddard (James Stewart) brought law and order to Shinbone, and an account of the real events in which his dirty work was done for him by an old friend (John Wayne), on the occasion of whose funeral the past is observed in flashback. On being presented with the true story, the local newspaper editor tears up the reporter's notes, saying: 'This is the West, sir. When the legend becomes fact, print the legend!' The editor's comment may be cynical, but Ford's presentation of the story is far from being so.

However, a total takeover by a countervailing realism either threatens to destroy the Western or replaces it with something new. Hamlin Garland's novels, for example, helped create a way of dealing with the pioneer experience which has little to do with the anterior traditions of the Western movie (in heroic saga, dime novel, stage melodrama); and so did Willa Cather and the Scandinavian-American novelist O. E. Rölvaag. Following their example the Swedish directors Bo Widerberg and Jan Troell have made films with Western settings but deliberately outside the framework of the conventional horse opera. Widerberg's highly uneven biography of the immigrant Swedish union organiser *Joe Hill* (1971) owes nothing to the Western, nor does *The Emigrants* (1971), the first of Troell's lengthy two-part adaptation of Vilhelm Moberg's fictional tetralogy concerning a group of peasants who left Sweden in the mid-1840s and settled in Minnesota. *Joe Hill* is a piece of political myth-making, a celebration of lyrical socialism after the manner of Widerberg's earlier *Ådalen '31*; *The Emigrants* is a calculatedly downbeat attempt to re-create with maximum fidelity an important area of the nineteenth-century proletarian experience. To be sure, their subject matter could easily have been rendered in terms of the traditional Western, but the directors have chosen to create their own truths and not to present them in refracted fashion through Hollywood convention, or in conscious contrast to a series of existing expectations, with a built-in resonance.

In this lies the partial failure of Troell and Widerberg. Their films stand alone. Whether American film-makers will follow their example remains to be seen. Unquestionably, there is a vast area of American history which falls outside the purview of the Western, but I doubt if it will prove all that rewarding. Robert Altman's *McCabe and Mrs Miller*, for instance, is a detailed, carefully thought out re-creation of pioneer life in a turn-of-the-century mining and timber settlement in Washington state. The central characters are the gambler McCabe (Warren Beatty) and his business partner, the skilled British cockney whore-cum-madame Mrs Miller (Julie Christie), and like the burgeoning frontier community which they exploit they are well within the framework of the Western movie.

For a long time, though, we learn more about the economics of the town than anything else: if earlier horse operas have educated us in gunplay and ranch management, Altman's picture is at times almost a U.S. Army Signals Corps instruction movie about setting up and running a brothel. We wonder indeed whether the film will actually become a Western at all. We are eventually reassured by a beautifully staged cold-blooded murder of an innocent cowboy who falls off a rope-bridge into a frozen river, and this is followed by a remarkably sustained running gunfight in the snow. We are reminded of *High Noon* as the frightened McCabe and the three killers, who have been despatched to put him out of business by an anonymous mining company, stalk each other round town. Indeed it is precisely because the film *is* a Western that Altman can confer a heroic status upon a seedy pimp and an opium-smoking whore – two simple, community-minded entrepreneurs standing up against the inexorable pressures of the faceless corporate state.

Two remarkable recent films, Sydney Pollack's *Jeremiah Johnson* (1972) and Robert Benton's *Bad Company* (1972), are also sustained rather than diminished by gradually turning

Gambler and madame: Julie Christie and Warren Beatty in Robert Altman's *McCab*
and Mrs Miller

into Westerns after opening sequences which could have take
them along the same trail as *The Emigrants* or *Joe Hill*. Th
central characters of both are fugitives from war. Whe
Jeremiah Johnson (Robert Redford) arrives in Colorado ter
ritory on the last fringe of civilisation during the 1840s, he i
still dressed in army uniform. Some years later, after painfull
re-creating himself as a self-sufficient Mountain Man, h
encounters a party of cavalry and asks them about the war –
is it over? The soldiers are momentarily taken aback by th
question: oh yes, the Mexican–American War, it's long over
and clearly almost forgotten. More explicitly, though not les
centrally, the band of teenagers led by the prissy middle-clas
farm boy Drew Dixon (Barry Brown) and the sharp, working
class Pennsylvanian Jake Rumsey (Jeff Bridges) in *Ba*
Company join forces in St Joseph, Missouri, and head West no
as pioneers but as draft-dodgers from the Civil War in 1863.

Traditionally in the movies and the more commercial aspects of popular culture, history and the past in general provide occasions for uplift rather than cynicism. The points of departure for *Jeremiah Johnson* and *Bad Company* are only too obviously a prevalent feeling about the Vietnam conflict, as are, of course, those for a number of other films I have mentioned earlier. But as the researches of the Chicago anthropologist Sol Tax have established, the Vietnam war was not uniquely unpopular in American history. Viewing the situation in 1968, Dr Tax placed Vietnam as only the fourth least popular war, coming behind the War of 1812, the Mexican War (1846–8), which was denounced from numerous quarters, by Lincoln, the Abolitionists and the Catholics, and the Civil War, which led to anti-draft riots infinitely bloodier than anything seen in twentieth-century America, and was termed 'a rich man's war and a poor man's fight'.[*]

In an interesting article twenty years ago in *Sight and Sound* (April–June 1953), written as the Korean War was drawing to a close, Herbert L. Jacobson argued that a renaissance of the cowboy picture took place during and immediately after World War II, and that the genre had played a key part in sustaining American military preparedness:

The seemingly miraculous transformation of the U.S. in two world wars from a people with practically no army and a buried, though glorious, military tradition, into a crushing military power, is due in no small part to the combative spirit kept alive in her youth by the cowboy tradition, itself constantly reflected in the American cinema . . .

In the light of much present-day thinking, such a comment sounds astonishingly naïve. Yet only on the surface do *Jeremiah Johnson* and *Bad Company* give the lie to it, and

---

[*] Quoted and discussed in *Rebellion on the Campus* by Seymour Martin Lipset (Routledge and Kegan Paul, London, 1972), p. 12.

precisely because their makers are so knowing, so sophisticated. Johnson is rejecting a corrupt Eastern American civilisation and its politics, but after a winter of discontent up snow-creek in search of a counter-culture without a copy of *The Last Whole Earth Catalogue*, he becomes a legendary figure, a murderous Indian fighter, though admittedly what triggers the change in his situation is the entry of the old world in the form of the U.S. cavalry, who force him into conflict with the Indians by making him commit the unforgivable sacrilege of crossing their ancient burial grounds. Nevertheless, what he has taken with him to the West is a scarcely containable inner violence which the immensity, the awesomeness of the land itself and its native inhabitants inevitably draw out. This is the D. H. Lawrence theme which in similar fashion underpins Mulligan's *The Stalking Moon*.

Jeremiah Johnson is high mimetic in character, and the grandeur of the scenery (mostly shot in winter) matches the grandiose aspirations of the director and his writers. *Bad Company* is low mimetic – at every point traditional heroism is undercut, as might be expected in the directorial debut of Robert Benton, who scripted the picture with David Newman, his co-screenwriter on *Bonnie and Clyde*. Never have the West and its inhabitants appeared more uninviting – the weather is invariably bad, the food is sparse, the windswept, treeless grass plains stretch endlessly on, a pilgrim making his way back East offers his wife's sexual services at a dollar a time, homesteaders charge exorbitant prices for inedible meals and a child gets the top of his head blown off for stealing a pie cooling on a window sill.

Bad Company is Tom Sawyer and Huck Finn out West, or perhaps even more a corrupt frontier version of *Oliver Twist* where the virtuous, hypocritical Drew plays Oliver to Jake Rumsey's Artful Dodger, and at the end the frame freezes on the two boys as they walk in with drawn pistols to rob their first Wells Fargo Office. The screen also freezes on Jeremiah

Johnson as he makes his final peace with the Indians. The fashionable device is the same in each film, but the meaning is different. True, both the Mountain Man and the pair of draft dodgers have become one with the land. But Johnson has been elevated to legendary status – he will ride off now up some frontier Olympus, freed by a violent transaction with the terrain and its remorseless guardians from his oppressive loneliness and selfhood. The boys in *Bad Company*, however, have been reduced – less perhaps at one with the land than with their society. They may be killed in the next minute, more likely they will meet their deaths in the succession of similar sordid robberies which will inevitably follow on from the present one. They have not transcended the violence of the world they sought to escape and which accompanied them to the West, but have gradually succumbed to it.

During the time I have been thinking about this book – roughly since 1963 when I began work on an uncompleted *Encounter* article looking at changes in the genre in the decade which had passed since Robert Warshow's famous essay in that journal – much has happened to the Western movie.

At that point Peckinpah's *Guns in the Afternoon* had just introduced the sight of indoor plumbing into a cowboy picture, something which in Vidor's *Man Without a Star* (1955) had been a matter for incredulous sniggering among the cowhands and which was not shown to the audience. Peckinpah went one further in *The Ballad of Cable Hogue* (1970) and presented a stagecoach driver loudly urinating in the desert. Not long after this, Joseph L. Mankiewicz in his first Western, *There Was a Crooked Man* (1970), staged a fight around the latrine in a frontier jail which concluded with the loser having his face ducked in a pool of urine. The floodgates, one might say, were then open: in *Monte Walsh* (1970) and *The Culpepper Cattle Company* (1972) the state of a cowboy's bowels becomes a matter of crucial dramatic importance. Other intimate aspects

Tom Sawyer and Huck Finn out West: Robert Benton's *Bad Company* (Jeff Bridges, Barry Brown)

of frontier life such as incest, homosexuality and masturbation (discussed at length in *McCabe and Mrs Miller*) have become, or are becoming, commonplace. These are perhaps minor matters, though not easily dismissed as being the products of prurience, titillation or a taste for spurious realism. Yet they should not distract attention from the way in which the Western has continued to dig away at the same old concerns, using a familiar range of situations and settings, and the way too that new Westerns make us look again at and revalue those which have gone before. Perhaps the final word on the interplay between convention, myth and reality should be Marianne Moore's prescription for poetry: 'imaginary gardens with real toads in them.' One must naturally be aware of the danger of being deceived by real gardens populated by plastic toads.

If I have a major fear about the future it is that, in Britain at least, there won't be enough places left to see Westerns in. As ate as the mid-Sixties a Londoner could find virtually all the postwar pictures mentioned in this book, up to that time, showing over a period of a couple of months on weekdays and at Sunday screenings at little back-street cinemas and suburban movie houses in a sort of permanent repertory. Such is no longer the case, nor will it ever be again. As I write this, the picture palace at the end of my road has put up its shutters forever. A few weeks before it closed I saw *When the Legends Die* there. Would that Stuart Millar's fine, elegiac film had been chosen, in the manner of Bogdanovich's *The Last Picture Show*, to end on — instead of letting the place die with the pathetic whimper of *Carry On Abroad*.

Back in 1962, in the high days of Kennedy's New Frontier, Fenin and Everson concluded their survey of over sixty years of Westerns with the sanguine comment:

It has been a distressingly long time now since such excellent Westerns as *Shane* and before it, *Wagonmaster*, *Stagecoach* and *The Toll Gate* appeared. But if a nation today can respond to the old values and spirit which made that nation great, then surely films will continue to be made by creative men depicting that history and the authenticity of the romance.

Even when I first read those words ten years ago, I had more faith in the Western than I had in Western society, from the complexity and doubts of which the movies have drawn their strength. While I am a good deal more optimistic than many about the future of America, I do feel that the health and renewal of the genre over the past decade suggests that its development does not necessarily depend upon the prosperity and confidence of the United States. Equally, I should be more than a little surprised if the enlarged Common Market, for all the countervailing economic and cultural force which it is expected to become, will produce in the foreseeable future a cinematic form drawing on our shared European history which is likely to challenge the Western.

Filmography

For the sake of convenience this selection of Westerns, most of them made since the end of World War II, is listed by directors. This does not mean that in all cases their importance or interest derives from their directors. Indeed, in many instances I would regard the contributions of screenwriters, actors, cinematographers and maybe even producers, as of greater significance. However, to annotate each individual picture adequately would possibly take up a book rather longer than the present one. The films rendered in capital letters are either personal favourites or have a particular value within the scheme of my monograph, or both.

Robert Aldrich: APACHE (1954); VERA CRUZ (1954); *The Last Sunset* (1961); *Four for Texas* (1963); ULZANA'S RAID (1972)

Robert Altman: *McCabe and Mrs Miller* (1971)

Robert Benton: *Bad Company* (1972)

Budd Boetticher: *The Cimarron Kid* (1951); *Horizons West* (1952); *Bronco Buster* (1952); *Seminole* (1953); *The Man from the Alamo* (1953); *Wings of the Hawk* (1953); SEVEN MEN FROM NOW (1956); THE TALL T (1957); *Decision at Sundown* (1957); *Buchanan Rides Alone* (1958); RIDE LONESOME (1959); *Westbound* (1959); COMANCHE STATION (1960); *A Time for Dying* (1969)

Marlon Brando: ONE EYED JACKS (1961)

Richard Brooks: THE LAST HUNT (1955); *The Professionals* (1966)

James B. Clark: *One Foot in Hell* (1960)

Fielder Cook: *A Big Hand for the Little Lady* (1966 – GB title, *Big Deal at Dodge City*)

George Cukor: HELLER IN PINK TIGHTS (1960)

Michael Curtiz: *Dodge City* (1939); *Virginia City* (1940); *Santa Fe Trail* (1940); *Jim Thorpe – All American* (1951 – GB title, *Man of Bronze*); *The Hangman* (1959); *The Comancheros* (1961)

Delmer Daves: BROKEN ARROW (1950); *Return of the Texan*

(1952); *Drumbeat* (1954); *Jubal* (1956); *The Last Wagon* (1956); 3.10 TO YUMA (1957); COWBOY (1958); *The Badlanders* (1958); THE HANGING TREE (1959)

André de Toth: *The Man in the Saddle* (1951); *Springfield Rifle* (1952); *Carson City* (1952); *The Stranger Wore a Gun* (1953); *Bounty Hunter* (1954); THE INDIAN FIGHTER (1955); *Riding Shotgun* (1955); DAY OF THE OUTLAW (1959)

Edward Dmytryk: BROKEN LANCE (1954); *Warlock* (1959); *Alvarez Kelly* (1966); *Shalako* (1969)

Gordon Douglas: *The Great Missouri Raid* (1952); *Only the Valiant* (1952); *The Charge at Feather River* (1953); *The Fiend that Walked the West* (1958); *Yellowstone Kelly* (1959); RIO CONCHOS (1964); *Stagecoach* (1966); *Chuka* (1967)

Allan Dwan: *The Woman They Almost Lynched* (1953); *Cattle Queen of Montana* (1954); *The Silver Lode* (1954); *Tennessee's Partner* (1955); *The Restless Breed* (1957)

Blake Edwards: *The Wild Rovers* (1971)

John Farrow: *California* (1947); *Copper Canyon* (1950); *Ride, Vaquero* (1953); HONDO (1954)

Richard Fleischer: *These Thousand Hills* (1959)

Peter Fonda: *The Hired Hand* (1971)

John Ford: STAGECOACH (1939); MY DARLING CLEMENTINE (1946); *Fort Apache* (1948); *Three Godfathers* (1948); *She Wore a Yellow Ribbon* (1949); WAGONMASTER (1950); *Rio Grande* (1950); THE SEARCHERS (1956); *The Horse Soldiers* (1959); *Sergeant Rutledge* (1960); *Two Rode Together* (1961); THE MAN WHO SHOT LIBERTY VALANCE (1961); *How the West Was Won* (1962, co-director); CHEYENNE AUTUMN (1964)

William Fraker: MONTE WALSH (1970)

Melvin Frank: *The Jayhawkers* (1959)

Hugo Fregonese: *Apache Drums* (1950); THE RAID (1954)

Samuel Fuller: *I Shot Jesse James* (1948); *The Baron of Arizona* (1949); RUN OF THE ARROW (1956); *Forty Guns* (1957)

Sidney J. Furie: *The Appaloosa* (1966 – GB title, *Southwest to Sonora*)

Tay Garnett: *Cattle King* (1963 – GB title, *Guns of Wyoming*)

Tom Gries: WILL PENNY (1967); *100 Rifles* (1968)

Charles Haas: STAR IN THE DUST (1956)

Henry Hathaway: *Rawhide* (1951); *Garden of Evil* (1954); FROM
HELL TO TEXAS (1958 – GB title, *Manhunt*); *North to Alaska*
(1960); *How the West Was Won* (1962 – co-director); THE
SONS OF KATIE ELDER (1965); *Nevada Smith* (1966);
5 Card Stud (1968); TRUE GRIT (1969); *Shoot Out* (1972)

Howard Hawks: RED RIVER (1948); *The Big Sky* (1952); RIO
BRAVO (1959); EL DORADO (1967); *Rio Lobo* (1970)

Monte Hellman: THE SHOOTING (1967); *Ride the Whirlwind*
(1967)

George Roy Hill: *Butch Cassidy and the Sundance Kid* (1969)

John Huston: *The Unforgiven* (1960); *The Misfits* (1960); *The Life
and Times of Judge Roy Bean* (1972)

Phil Karlson: GUNMAN'S WALK (1958); *A Time for Killing*
(1968 – British title, *The Long Ride Home*)

Burt Kennedy: *Mail Order Bride* (1964 – GB title, *West of
Montana*); *The Rounders* (1965); *Return of the Seven* (1966);
WELCOME TO HARD TIMES (1966 – GB title, *Killer on a
Horse*); *The War Wagon* (1967); *Support Your Local Sheriff*
(1968); *Young Billy Young* (1969); THE GOOD GUYS AND
THE BAD GUYS (1969); *Dirty Dingus Magee* (1970); *The
Deserter* (1970); *Hannie Caulder* (1971); *Support your Local
Gunfighter* (1971); *The Train Robbers* (1973)

Henry King: *Jesse James* (1939); THE GUNFIGHTER (1950);
The Bravados (1958)

Fritz Lang: *The Return of Frank James* (1940); *Western Union*
(1941); RANCHO NOTORIOUS (1952)

J. Lee Thompson: *Mackenna's Gold* (1969)

Sergio Leone: *A Fistful of Dollars* (1964); *For a Few Dollars More*
(1965); *The Good, the Bad and the Ugly* (1967); *Once Upon a
Time in the West* (1969); *A Fistful of Dynamite* (1971)

Henry Levin: *The Man from Colorado* (1948); *The Lonely Man*
(1957)

Joseph H. Lewis: *The Halliday Brand* (1957); *Terror in a Texas
Town* (1957)

Joseph L. Mankiewicz: *There Was a Crooked Man* (1970)

Anthony Mann: DEVIL'S DOORWAY (1950); WINCHESTER
'73 (1950); *The Furies* (1950); *Bend of the River* (1952 – GB
title, *Where the River Bends*); THE NAKED SPUR (1953); *The*

ward Hawks' *Red River* (John Wayne, Montgomery Clift)

Far Country (1955); *The Man from Laramie* (1955); THE LAST
FRONTIER (1956); *The Tin Star* (1957); MAN OF THE
WEST (1958); *Cimarron* (1960)

orge Marshall: *Destry Rides Again* (1939); *The Savage* (1952);
Red Garters (1954); THE SHEEPMAN (1958); *How the West
Was Won* (1962 – co-director); *Advance to the Rear* (1964 – GB
title, *Company of Cowards*)

ncent McEveety: FIRECREEK (1968)

on McGuire: *Johnny Concho* (1956)

ndrew V. McLaglen: *Gun the Man Down* (1956); *McLintock!*
(1963); *Shenandoah* (1965); *The Rare Breed* (1966); *The Way
West* (1967); *Bandolero!* (1968); *The Undefeated* (1969); *Chisum*
(1970); *One More Train to Rob* (1971); *Something Big* (1971)

ay Milland: *A Man Alone* (1955)

uart Millar: WHEN THE LEGENDS DIE (1972)

avid Miller: *Lonely Are the Brave* (1962)

len H. Miner: *Black Patch* (1957); THE RIDE BACK (1957)

obert Mulligan: THE STALKING MOON (1968)

lvio Narizzano: *Blue* (1968)

James Neilson: *Night Passage* (1957); *Return of the Gunfighter* (196(

Ralph Nelson: *Duel at Diablo* (1965); *Soldier Blue* (1970)

Joseph M. Newman: *The Outcasts of Poker Flat* (1952); *Th* *Gunfight at Dodge City* (1959); *A Thunder of Drums* (1961)

Gerd Oswald: *The Brass Legend* (1955); *Fury at Showdown* (1956)

Robert Parrish: *Saddle the Wind* (1958); THE WONDERFUL COUNTRY (1959)

Sam Peckinpah: THE DEADLY COMPANIONS (1961); RID THE HIGH COUNTRY (1962 – GB title, *Guns in th Afternoon*); MAJOR DUNDEE (1965); THE WILD BUNCH (1969); *The Ballad of Cable Hogue* (1970); JUNIOR BONNE (1972); *Pat Garrett and Billy the Kid* (1973)

Arthur Penn: THE LEFT-HANDED GUN (1958); LITTLE BIG MAN (1970)

Frank Perry: *Doc* (1971)

Sydney Pollack: *The Scalphunters* (1968); *Jeremiah Johnson* (1972

Abraham Polonsky: TELL THEM WILLIE BOY IS HERE (1969

Otto Preminger: RIVER OF NO RETURN (1954)

Ted Post: *The Legend of Tom Dooley* (1959); *Hang 'Em High* (196

Nicholas Ray: *The Lusty Men* (1952); JOHNNY GUITAR (1953 *Run for Cover* (1954); THE TRUE STORY OF JESSE JAME (1956 – GB title, *The James Brothers*)

Carol Reed: *Flap* (1970 – GB title, *The Last Warrior*)

Dick Richards: THE CULPEPPER CATTLE COMPANY (1972

Martin Ritt: HUD (1963); *The Outrage* (1964); HOMBRE (1967

Cliff Robertson: *J. W. Coop* (1971)

Russell Rouse: *The Fastest Gun Alive* (1956); *Thunder in the S* (1959)

Mark Rydell: *The Cowboys* (1972)

Sidney Salkow: *Sitting Bull* (1954)

Harold Schuster: THE DRAGOON WELLS MASSACRE (1957

George Sidney: *The Harvey Girls* (1946)

Don Siegel: *Duel at Silver Creek* (1952); FLAMING STAR (196(COOGAN'S BLUFF (1968); *Death of a Gunfighter* (1969 credited to 'Allen Smithee' but directed by Robert Totten and D Siegel); *Two Mules for Sister Sara* (1969)

Elliot Silverstein: CAT BALLOU (1965); A MAN CALLE HORSE (1970) ert Siodmak: *Custer of the West* (1967)

glas Sirk: *Taza, Son of Cochise* (1954)

rge Stevens: SHANE (1953); *Giant* (1956)

n Sturges: *The Walking Hills* (1949); *Escape from Fort Bravo*
1953); BAD DAY AT BLACK ROCK (1954); *Backlash* (1955);
unfight at the O.K. Corral (1957); THE LAW AND JAKE
ADE (1958); *Last Train from Gun Hill* (1959); THE MAGNI-
ICENT SEVEN (1960); *Sergeants Three* (1961); *The Hallelujah
rail* (1965); HOUR OF THE GUN (1967); *Joe Kidd* (1972)

ry Thorpe: DAY OF THE EVIL GUN (1968)

ques Tourneur: *Stranger on Horseback* (1955); WICHITA
1955); *Great Day in the Morning* (1956)

ar G. Ulmer: *The Naked Dawn* (1954)

g Vidor: *Billy the Kid* (1930); *The Texas Rangers* (1936); *North
West Passage* (1939); DUEL IN THE SUN (1946); MAN
WITHOUT A STAR (1955)

ul Walsh: THEY DIED WITH THEIR BOOTS ON (1941);
Pursued (1947); *Silver River* (1948); *Colorado Territory* (1949);
Along the Great Divide (1950); *Distant Drums* (1951); *The
Lawless Breed* (1952); *Gun Fury* (1953); THE TALL MEN
1955); *The King and Four Queens* (1956); *The Sheriff of
Fractured Jaw* (1959); A DISTANT TRUMPET (1963)

arles Marquis Warren: *Hellgate* (1952); ARROWHEAD (1954);
Tension at Table Rock (1956); *Trooper Hook* (1957)

n Wayne: THE ALAMO (1960)

bert D. Webb: THE PROUD ONES (1956)

lliam A. Wellman: THE OX-BOW INCIDENT (1942 – GB title,
Strange Incident); *Yellow Sky* (1948); *Across the Wide Missouri*
1951); *Westward the Women* (1952)

l Wendkos: *Face of a Fugitive* (1959)

chard Wilson: *The Man with a Gun* (1955 – GB title, *The Trouble
Shooter*); INVITATION TO A GUNFIGHTER (1964)

chael Winner: *Lawman* (1971); *Chato's Land* (1972)

bert Wise: *Blood on the Moon* (1948); *Two Flags West* (1950);
Tribute to a Bad Man (1956)

lliam Wyler: *The Westerner* (1940); *Friendly Persuasion* (1956);
THE BIG COUNTRY (1958)

d Zinnemann: HIGH NOON (1952)

Bibliography

The best, most easily available book on the West is the late John A
Hawgood's *The American West* (Eyre and Spottiswoode, Londor
1967, published in the United States by Knopf as *America's Wester
Frontiers*). This is far and away the most comprehensive single wor
on the subject and contains a first-class bibliographical note whic
covers all the available literature up to that time. Of the hundreds c
books Hawgood mentions, I feel it necessary to underline the import
ance to the serious student of the Western of Henry Nash Smith'
remarkable essay on 'The American West as Symbol and Myth
Virgin Land (1950). All British students of the West are in debt t
Hawgood for his own scrupulous scholarship and for his editorshi
of Eyre and Spottiswoode's 'Frontier Library'.

As indicated in the text, I have found numerous books not strictl
concerned with the West of great value – Howard Mumford Jone
O Strange New World (Chatto and Windus, London, 1965); John W
McCoubrey's *American Tradition in Painting* (George Brazille
New York, 1963); as well as several books by the late Richar
Hofstadter, most particularly *Anti-Intellectualism in American Lif*
(1963) and *The Progressive Historians* (1968). Professor Hawgood'
bibliography encompasses the principal texts on American Indian
but since then there has been a sizeable body of work which nobod
interested in the subject should neglect: Alvin Josephy's *The India
Heritage of America* (1968); *The American Indian Today*, edited b
Stuart Little and Nancy O. Lurie (revised edition, 1968); *Ou
Brother's Keeper*, edited by Edgar S. Cahn (1969); Dee Brown'
Bury My Heart at Wounded Knee (1971); and the three ke
polemical texts by Vine Deloria Jr – *Custer Died For Your Sin*
(1969), *We Talk, You Listen* (1970), and *Of the Utmost Good Fait*
(1971).

174

he principal general book-length studies of the Western are:

gel, Henri (editor), *Le Western* (Études Cinématographiques 12–13, Lettres Modernes, Paris, 1961, revised and updated by Jean A. Gili, 1969)

ellour, Raymond (editor) *Le Western: Sources, Mythes, Auteurs, Acteurs, Filmographies* (Le Monde en 10/18, Union Générale d'Editions, Paris, 1966, revised, 1968)

yles, Allen, *The Western: An Illustrated Guide* (A. Zwemmer, London; A. S. Barnes, New York, 1967). This little handbook is an accurate and fairly comprehensive index, invaluable to the student of the genre. A revised edition is overdue, and would be welcome.

enin, George N. and Everson, William K., *The Western: From Silents to Cinerama* (The Orion Press, New York, 1962)

ord, Charles, *Histoire du Western* (Editions Pierre Horay, Paris, 1964)

arkinson, Michael and Jeavons, Clyde, *A Pictorial History of Westerns* (Hamlyn, London, 1972)

ieupeyrout, Jean-Louis, *La Grande Aventure du Western* (Editions du Cerf, Paris, 1971). This is the most ambitious book on the subject, a greatly extended and enlarged version of Rieupeyrout's 1953 book *Le Western*, which contained a preface by André Bazin subsequently reprinted in the third volume of Bazin's *Qu'est-ce que le Cinéma?* (1961)

here have appeared in recent years several studies of individual irectors of which the best, and most germane, is Jim Kitses' *Horizons West* (Thames and Hudson, London, 1969), also a 'Cinema One' book, which deals admirably and lucidly, if somewhat olemnly, with the Westerns of Anthony Mann, Budd Boetticher and am Peckinpah. In his 'Cinema One' monograph on *Howard Hawks* Secker and Warburg, London, 1968), Robin Wood analyses with haracteristic insight Hawks' *Red River*, *Rio Bravo* and *El Dorado*. *eter Bogdanovich's *John Ford* (Studio Vista, London, 1967), irgely devoted to an unsearching interview, is full of information; ohn Baxter's *The Cinema of John Ford* (A. Zwemmer, London; A. . Barnes, New York, 1972) complements it with shrewd criticism.

The periodical literature on the Western, both in general and specialised journals, is immense and continually growing. Th indexes of any of the world's leading film magazines will reve numerous articles, interviews and reviews. I will content myself he with a list of five interesting pieces not aimed initially at movie fans:

Barr, Charles, 'Western', *Axle Quarterly* No. 3 (London, 1963)

Gregory, Horace, 'Guns of the Roaring West', in *Avon Book o Modern Writing No. 2*, edited by William Phillips and Philip Rah (Avon Publications, New York, 1954)

Kitchen, Laurence, 'Decline of the Western', *The Listener* (London 14 July, 1966)

Schein, Harry, 'Den Olympiske Cowboyen', *Bonniers Litterär Magasin* (Stockholm, January, 1954), translated as 'The Olympi Cowboy', *The American Scholar* (Summer, 1955)

Warshow, Robert, 'Movie Chronicle: The Westerner', *Partisa Review*, March–April, 1954, reprinted in *Encounter* (March, 1954 as 'The Gentleman with a Gun', and included in Warshow's *Th Immediate Experience* (Doubleday, New York, 1962).

Acknowledgments

I am grateful to Penelope Houston, Tom Milne, James Price and David Wilson for their encouragement and patience over the longish period during which I have been intermittently engaged in writing this book.

Part of the first chapter and the section on Indians have appeared in somewhat different form in, respectively, *The Times* and *Art in America* and are reprinted by permission o their editors.

Stills by courtesy of Avco Embassy, Cinerama, Columbia, Ember, MGM, Paramount, Rank, 20th Century-Fox, United Artists, Warner Bros., and the Stills Library of the National Film Archive, London.

This book is dedicated to my late father, who took me to my first Western, and to Sean, Patrick and Karl, who saw their firs Westerns with me.